MURDER ON THE MARSH

JOHN FERGUSON

First published: London, 1930

This edition published 2022 by

OREON

an imprint of

The Oleander Press
16 Orchard Street
Cambridge
CB1 1JT

www.oleanderpress.com

A CIP catalogue record for the book
is available from the British Library.

ISBN: 9781915475183

Cover design, typesetting & ebook: neorelix

The language and views expressed herein are those of a
bygone era and, whilst probably obvious, it should still
be noted that they are not shared by this publisher.

MURDER ON THE MARSH

Thank you very much for buying
this title from OREON

Sign up to our infrequent newsletter
to receive a **free** copy of
Fatality in Fleet Street
by Christopher St John Sprigg and get
news of new titles, discounts and give-aways!

https://www.oleanderpress.com/golden-age-crime.html

Chapter 1

At first the case did not seem to me worthy of Francis McNab's attention. And still less did it look like developing into an affair on which the *Daily Record* would soon splash into its heaviest triple headlines. The affair, that is, promised nothing of that keen intellectual excitement which drew out McNab's energies, nor had it any of those picturesque or sensational qualities which, properly worked up, make a million readers scramble for their morning newspaper. The Romney Marsh mystery, one of the most diabolically ingenious murders in criminal records, began, in fact, like a little cloud, no bigger than a man's hand rising out of the sea, formless as a breath, unsubstantial as a dream.

But well do I remember the day on which it began to take shape and substance. Matheson, my chief on the *Record*, called me up to his den about four o'clock. When I entered he was seated at his writing table with the galley proofs of McNab's weekly crime article in his hand. It was plain to see he was in one of his black moods. He almost flung the article at me.

"Too abstract again," he snapped. "Crime in the concrete is what interests: if he will be abstract he must be brief. Take this round when you finish, and get him to cut it by a third."

I knew what he meant. McNab, when not writing on some actual baffling crime that clamoured for solution, was inclined to be too scientific, too philosophic and psychological in catering for our readers.

"Of course," I said, taking over the crumpled proof, "there isn't any big thing for him to write about at the moment."

But Matheson, who had already pivoted his chair round to take up other work, received my remark in silence. After staring at the back of his bullet head for a moment I turned to the door, but he pulled me up before I reached it.

"Oh – er – Chance," he drawled over his shoulder, "Williams returns from his holidays on Friday, so you can have your fortnight from then."

This was better. Week by week I had seen the summer slip away, and always it was someone else's turn. Now we were in the second week of September. Still, the glory of summer had not yet fled. So, after collecting some letters that had come in for McNab, I made for the Adelphi by way of the Embankment, just to sample, as it were, the feeling of freedom that would be mine on the next Friday. And the first thing my eye took note of was that the leaves were yet unfaded on the trees. But, from speculating on my holiday as I walked along, I soon turned to wonder how McNab would receive Matheson's request. Never before had I carried such a message to him. Well I knew what Matheson wanted for the paper, for it was what I wanted myself – more of those brilliant comments on some topical crime then baffling the police which he contributed to the *Record* under his *nom de plume* of "The Lamplighter." But such a demand at that moment was, as I had indicated to Matheson, like asking McNab to make bricks without straw. For no unsolved crime then occupied the public mind. This had happened before, of course; and, when it did, McNab occasionally turned his pen on to crimes not yet tabulated as crimes in the statute books; particularly did he like to illuminate the career of some rogue not recognised as such, who, having attained wealth, was looking confidently forward to a title. Matheson, however, had always eyed such articles with dubiety, much preferring that McNab should deal with the type of criminal who got punished rather than rewarded. And there again I agreed with Matheson.

But there was something I now liked much better than any sort of writing about crime, and that was contact with an actual criminal that had the thrill of danger in it. To see Francis McNab's penetrative mind at work, to see him at full stretch in the solution of some hidden crime that had its origin in the dark corridors of human passion, to be with him when he picked up the scent, forced the human fox into the open, followed and cornered him, that was the real thing. And I had known the difference ever since my association with McNab in that queer Lady Wye affair. Journalist though I was, it was not crime in black and white, but crime in the red and white, so to speak, that gripped me after that experience.

Well, most of this I was making clear to myself as I walked along the Embankment in the gathering dusk of the serene and mellow September day. Somewhere behind Westminster the setting sun showed as a translucent golden haze against which the ugly Charing Cross bridge in the foreground stretched like a heavy purple shadow across the lambent waters. The sight started me off considering what to do with my approaching holiday. What does one do with a fortnight in September?

I knew well what I should like to do. To be up to the neck in another case with McNab, this time free from Matheson's claim on my time and all sense of responsibility for getting stuff for the *Record* out of the case; that would be my choice. But I fancied McNab had no big case in hand just then unless, I said to myself, there should be a case in one or other of the letters I was then carrying to him. Not that it was likely.

Many letters addressed to "The Lamplighter" came from readers of McNab's articles, but only about one in a thousand led to anything; and not one of them had so far ever led up to anything big. Still, as I turned up Villiers Street I looked at those now in my hand, speculating on the possibility. There were six letters, and the postmarks showed me that they came from Rotherham, Cardiff, Haywards Heath, Manchester and New Romney, the postmark of the sixth being indecipherable. The fifth took my eye for the simple reason that I remembered a letter from the same place and in similar feminine handwriting which had come in for McNab a few days previously.

All the letters, except one, appeared to come from women. Nothing to hope for from them, I thought; for I knew the sort of things they would contain. Mostly they came in after some petty crime in the writer's neighbourhood, and suggested that, if all were known, the culprit would be found to be so and so; and it took no great powers of penetration to see that the name given was that of a neighbouring lady against whom the anonymous writer had an obvious grudge.

But, by the look of it, I felt sure the Haywards Heath letter did not come from a lady. The bold handwriting fairly bristled like serried lines of bayonets. A colonel, I said to myself, who has discovered a Bolshevist plot hatching out on the Sussex Downs perhaps, but at least not a lady who has unearthed a plot among the neighbours against the life of her gentle Alsatian. This was the one letter on which any faint hope could be based. And so I felt as, having mounted to the flat in the Adelphi, I rang the familiar bell.

McNab was sprawling, relaxed, in his low wicker chair. He had evidently been reading, but in the failing light had left off and laid the book face downwards on his knees. This did not look as if he had anything in hand that would fill my holiday with interest and excitement.

"Taken to novel reading?" I remarked, handing him the letters. "What is it, a detective story?" And, as he made no answer while scanning the letters, I added with a sigh, "I suppose it is the next best thing to being in a case oneself." Then, catching sight of the title, I could not repress a groan; the book was *Alice's Adventures in Wonderland*.

"A work of science, not a novel," McNab said, without looking up from the letters, and so not perceiving that I knew what the volume was. No doubt he didn't like being caught reading such a book. But I could have groaned again as I saw how little he must have on hand if he were reduced to reading such a childish book. And yet he looked fatigued, as if he had been all day out on some pressing work. Could it be that he was merely relaxing for the moment, and that he had a big case in hand? But when I put the question he only shook his head.

I watched to see which of the letters he would open first. He sat up suddenly, the book slipping to the floor, and ripped open, not the Haywards Heath communication, as I was betting with myself he would, but the one with the New Romney postmark. The frown deepened on his face as he read.

"Innisbuie!" He breathed his favourite Gaelic expletive. What the word meant I did not know. But when he laid the pink sheet on his knee thoughtfully I slipped it out of his slack fingers while he appeared to be pondering its contents. This is what I read:

>
> REDCOTES
> NEAR NEW ROMNEY
> KENT
> Monday

Dear Sir,

Many many thanks for your letter with the kind advice to me. I am *certain* the fault is mine that I failed to make myself clear in my last letter. It is *so* difficult to put things in writing. So as you *have* misunderstood me I write to say that I am *venturing* to ask you to see me when I come to London on Wednesday, I have looked up the trains and as far as I can make out it *ought* to be about seven when I call on you. *Please* do not reply to this as it might lead to complications here which *might* make it impossible for me to get away.

Yours sincerely,

A. Cardew

It gratified me to see, from various features in the letter, that I had been right in my guess at the sex of the writer. But I could see no promise of an interesting case here.

"Well, Godfrey, what do you make of it?" McNab said, eyeing me.

"Another request for an investigation into the strange disappearance of a favourite cat?" I hazarded in disgust.

"And the writer?" he asked, beginning to open the other letters.

"An idle, brainless old maid with no sense of proportion."

"You're probably right about the sex, and her condition – she writes so breathlessly – but why do you call her brainless?"

"Well, isn't it obvious, if she gets flurried over the loss of a pussy cat?"

"But I didn't say it was a cat."

"Well, a Peke or a Pom – something tame, anyhow, the value of which she exaggerates because it belongs to herself."

This inference of mine was not so absurd as might be supposed, for a large proportion of the letters McNab received through our office came from dear, silly old ladies who regarded him indeed as a genius, a genius with an infinite capacity for taking pains over their trifles. Indeed, all the letters I had brought seemed to be of the same futile character, for I observed that he now laid them down with a yawn.

"Get me the C file from the cabinet," he said. "You'd better have all the known facts, and then we can spend the time of waiting by testing your progress in deductive processes."

He may have been laughing at me; but my thought, as I went to the file cabinet was that, anyway, there was more sense in this than in reading *Alice in Wonderland*.

When I handed him the section wanted he picked out a letter which was written on the same pink-coloured paper as the New Romney one we had been discussing. He read it through very slowly, as it seemed to me, apparently reconsidering its contents in the light of the writer's second letter. I recalled that the lady had loudly asserted she had been misunderstood. It seemed to worry McNab. Finally he shook his head and passed the letter to me.

A. Cardew's original letter was longer than the one I had already read; but, though the femininity was just as discernible, there was less fluttering agitation in it.

REDCOTES
NEAR NEW ROMNEY
KENT

Dear Sir,

Will you pardon one who is a stranger to you addressing you on a very serious matter? The truth is, however, that you do not seem a stranger to me. This is because I have for some time been reading your articles in the *Daily Record*, after hearing them discussed at a house near here where I chanced to be at tea. So, when the thing I am about to tell you of happened, I always felt that if the worst should threaten I had you to consult. And now the time has come. But I had better begin at the beginning.

On arriving home from Paris last June I found my father greatly changed. He is a very old man now, greatly changed. When he met me at the station I hardly knew him, and he hardly seemed pleased to see me. That was the first shock, and during the drive home, while I was telling all my news, he seemed to be thinking of something else, and when I asked questions about his pedigree Guernseys and what had been happening at home, he answered me just anything, at random. I was very unhappy. Then I told myself it was just a mood, and he would be alright [*sic*] in the morning. But he wasn't. And he has been like that ever since.

Of course I knew there was something far wrong. At first I thought it was his health. But when I tried to question him he became impatient, and said I mustn't be fanciful. After that I could see he tried to brighten up and be cheerful like he used to be, but it was all forced work, and very distressing to see, and though I pretended to be convinced there was nothing amiss with him I kept watching him all the time.

Then a few weeks ago I got near to finding out what it was. Not his health at all, but something else troubled him. I found out two things. First, he is afraid of something or someone who comes into the garden at night. Second, that he is more afraid sometimes on Wednesdays and always on Tuesday nights than on any other, though every night now he sleeps with his window shut and bolted. But ever since I surprised him watching the garden from the staircase window he knows I suspect something, and now he watches me just like I watch him. But it can't go on; it can't, it can't. Please, *please*, you who see so deep into things, if it is true you do, tell me what to do.

Yours very truly,

A. Cardew

McNab looked over as I folded the letter.

"Well, you who see so deeply into things, what did you make of it?" I asked.

While fumbling for his cigarette case he replied:

"It was to see what you can make of it I asked you to get that letter."

"Because it is a nice easy one. I must say you don't flatter me there."

"Easy, is it? All right, proceed."

Crossing his extended legs, he lit his cigarette. I re-read the letter carefully. When I looked up again his eyes were on me. With fairness I could now plead that he himself had had several days in which to consider its contents. But it all seemed very simple to me.

"This old gentleman," I began, "has obviously developed heart trouble which he is concealing from an over-anxious, worrying daughter of mature years who has developed an over-suspicious mind through reading your articles in the *Record*. That concealment of his, and your crime articles, have set her unbalanced mind into a flutter; otherwise she would know it is not a detective she should call in, but a doctor."

McNab elevated his chin to blow out a big spiral of smoke.

"Heart trouble, you think? But how does that square with her finding him watching something outside in the garden from the staircase window?"

"Squares perfectly," I asserted. "The poor old fellow was resting halfway up the stairs on his way to bed. He would naturally put both hands on the sill of the staircase window as a convenient support. He would be rather breathless too. But to the overheated imagination of this fussy daughter, watchfully peering down at him over the banisters, he would seem to be looking through the window in great agitation."

"But she mentions this as happening always on Tuesdays and on Wednesdays occasionally. Why should her imagination, or his heart, palpitate only on those nights?"

This left me helpless for the moment.

"Aha!" McNab nodded. "That leaves you scratching your head, does it? Well, it puzzled me for a time. The key, you know, lies in that reference to the pedigree Guernseys."

"The pedigree Guernseys?" I echoed. "What on earth have they—"

He held up a hand.

"Wait! Let's straighten out the situation from the start. To begin with, why do you conclude that A. Cardew is a woman?"

"That isn't a thing one has to arrive at a conclusion about," I said stoutly. "It jumps to the eye; it is all over the letters somehow. I defy anyone to read them and not know the sex of the writer."

"Let that pass then. But why did you say she is of mature years?"

"Because she described her father as a very old man."

"But her words tell you absolutely nothing about his age."

"I don't follow you there."

"To any girl under twenty, forty seems to verge on decrepitude. So you cannot accept her description of her father as correct till you know her own age."

But about this I could, from the facts given, be dogmatic enough.

"She's no chit of a girl, anyhow."

"Why?

"Been living in Paris, apparently alone."

"And from that you infer just how much more?"

"That her family is comfortably off, that she probably speaks French, and is, at the very least, sufficiently mature to look after herself."

"But not after her father?"

With difficulty I kept a grip on the argument after this thrust.

"That's different. Call the modern girl what you like, you can't call her, as this woman is, morbid on health matters, least of all about her parents."

"And, therefore, you conclude – ?"

"That, as this A. Cardew is obviously excitable, fanciful and fantastically apprehensive of imaginary dangers, she is clearly of that older generation which wore chest protectors and used to look under the bed for burglars every night. She's certainly not under forty."

"And that would put her father's age at what?"

"In the middle sixties at least – old enough to have developed a heart," I cut in, rather well pleased with my reasoning since I appeared to have carried McNab with me.

"A heart from which he suffers regularly on Tuesdays and occasionally on Wednesdays," he remarked thoughtfully.

Now I saw he had been quizzing me. I had overlooked those Tuesdays and Wednesdays and what they implied. He grinned at my discomfiture, then sighed with exaggerated plaintiveness.

"Will you never learn to put two and two together?" he said with affected weariness. "You still overlook that reference to the pedigree Guernseys."

"But," I protested, "I don't know what a pedigree Guernsey is – rabbit, or hen, or dog."

"Cow!" he snapped, much as if the word were an abusive epithet addressed to myself.

"Oh, all right. But I don't see how I can put Tuesdays and Wednesdays and Guernsey cows together and make anything out of the combination. You might as well talk of putting two o'clock and three red herrings together – there's no sense in it."

For a moment I thought I had him cornered.

Throwing away his cigarette, as if the taste had suddenly displeased him, he lay back in the chair, clasping both hands behind his head. That I should have scored one over McNab, above all on a point in logic, was no small triumph for me. For, trivial as this discussion was, merely intended to pass the time while waiting for A. Cardew's arrival, I was well enough aware that to McNab nothing that even remotely touched on his profession could be trivial.

At length he broke the silence.

"When we know his occupation it's easy to put them together."

This looked like hedging.

"But, unfortunately, that, with a lot more, the lady omitted to tell us."

"She did," McNab admitted. "Still, all the same, the information is in the letter. You missed it, that is all. Her anxiety is, of course, caused by the old man's journeys to Ashford and Rye."

"But," I protested, "she doesn't even mention Ashford or Rye. If you have more information which you are keeping up your sleeve, I don't see how—"

"These two letters contain all I know," he cut in, adding, "but it is all there, his occupation and age, his habits, his real malady, and so on, if only you would use your wits. Why is it that people who can put two and two together with figures hardly ever think of doing so with facts?"

I didn't like the over-emphatic sigh he here produced, and said bluntly:

"Well, anyway, I'm still waiting to see you put those Tuesdays and Wednesdays and the Guernsey cows together."

McNab sat forward, resting his chin on the hollow of his hand.

"It's all in that," he said, "in her mention of the pedigree Guernseys, I mean. But there's even more significance in the way she referred to them on that drive home with her father. Finding him strange in manner, and absent-minded, she seeks for something to kindle his interest, to rouse him out of himself; and clearly her thought was that the Guernseys would do that. Obviously she chose them as the most sure subject to interest him. Does it not follow that if the raising of pedigree stock is not his occupation he is at least a man keenly interested in it? Very well, that hint is enough to go on with. I take up my Automobile Association handbook. A glance at the map shows me that the nearest towns in the neighbourhood likely to have market days are Hythe, Ashford, Tenterden and Rye. I turn these places up, and find that, while Hythe and Tenterden have not a market day, Ashford and Rye both have, and that there is a market at Ashford every Tuesday, and at Rye every alternate Wednesday."

Light dawned on me.

"Sometimes on Wednesdays and always on Tuesdays,' "I quoted. "Yes, it seems conclusive. The old fellow attends the markets, and comes home exhausted. On his way to bed she sees him stop halfway upstairs, apparently staring breathlessly through the staircase window into the black night. So she jumps to the old-maidish conclusion that he fears attack from outside. That is to say, she easily observes all the visible effects of his trouble, but is mistaken about the invisible cause, that is all."

McNab relaxed again, glancing at his watch as he stretched his legs.

"That is that," he said. "But we'll have to see the lady before we can say it is all."

"Well," I said after a moment's thought, "with all your reasoning you have only reached the conclusion I reached at the start. She's just a poor old thing with a bee in her bonnet."

"One of the conclusions you *jumped at*," he corrected.

"And she probably does wear a bonnet, coming from an outlandish place like that – a black bonnet with jingling jet ornaments," I added.

He did not seem to hear me.

"If anything does lie behind, as yet unknown to us, you might do worse than go down with her to investigate," he suggested.

But the startled glance I shot at him let me see he was not serious; there was mirth in his eyes, though his features were solemn enough. Still, I knew it was only because he felt there was nothing in the case that the mirth was in his eyes. For he was quite capable of sending me off in the company of any old woman if he had even a doubt about her case. He could be so nice to elderly females. In some of his ideas he was quite Victorian. Perhaps it would be safer, I thought, to make my position clear now, lest the interview with her should modify his opinions about the affair. I had no intention of wasting my fortnight in that fashion. The mere thought of the possibility made me hot.

"Look here, McNab," I began warmly, "if you think I am going to squander my hard-earned holiday in the company of an old—"

He cut me short.

"Wheesht, man, didn't you hear the bell?"

There came a tap on the door, and the next moment the old housekeeper popped her grizzled head inside.

"There's a leddy o' the name o' Cardew asking for you, sir. She says she's an appintment."

McNab, nodding assent, rose alertly.

"Quite right. Show the young lady in," he said.

Chapter 2

AT sight of the figure which stood in the doorway I felt a sudden flurry of irritation against McNab. All along he had somehow known she was young, and had kept the fact to himself, gravely leading me on, to make me look foolish with my false inferences and deductions. I ought to have profited by former experiences. But McNab's notions of humour differed radically from my own, and his face was no help, except that it always looked most serious when he was trying to be funny. This was, in fact, one of those cautious Scotch traits in him that I heartily disliked. But, as I used to say to myself, while trying to subdue my irritation, it was a racial rather than a personal defect in McNab. That solemn face in the humorous moment, peculiar to every Scot, is due to the fact that no Scot likes to give anything away, himself not the least. And so the solemn face at the humorous moment merely means that if the humour misses fire, or falls flat, he is not made to look foolish.

And probably it was the foolish look of surprise on my face that made Miss Cardew, after one glance at me, address herself to McNab.

"You are Lamplighter."

It was an assertion more than a question. McNab assented, offering his hand, which she took quickly, as people do when such an offer comes unexpectedly. I fancy she held on to his hand, as if, at last, getting a grip on something that helped her, while still keeping her eyes almost hungrily on his face.

"If you can throw any light on – on – dark places..." she said with a shiver.

McNab disengaged his hand to indicate a chair at the far end of the room.

"Come over here and tell us all about it," he said.

At this her dark eyes turned on me doubtfully.

"Mr. Chance, of the *Record*," McNab explained, as I crossed to shut the window. "He assists me occasionally. Though, of course, if you prefer that he should go—"

The spasm of apprehension which McNab's malicious suggestion gave me was relieved by the girl's hasty interruption:

"No, no. I am quite sure it is all right."

She sat rather on the edge of her chair; and while McNab was putting some trivial questions about her journey, questions designed to set her more at her ease, I was able to have a good look at her. The first impression she made on me was so vivid, simply, I think, because I had so completely to revise the preconception I had formed from her two letters. She was a slight little thing, looking, in the close-fitting blue coat which did not quite cover her knees when seated, not more than twenty. Hardly as much, in fact, as she sat forward on the edge of her chair, her face uplifted, replying to McNab's trivial questions with the eager promptitude of a young girl anxious to please. But the over-brightness in the dark eyes and the pallor of the finely-drawn face betrayed the prolonged torture and anxiety which had made her turn to us for help.

Of course I knew that McNab's questions about the Romney Marsh, and its breed of sheep and cattle, and its climate, were not so purposeless as they must have seemed to anyone else. Either, I told myself, he is probing for symptoms of hysteria, or testing her general mental capacity, to see just how far he can trust her judgment. But certainly some of the questions he put with so simple an air, especially those on the geography of the

Marsh, were such as might have been put to a schoolgirl. Some impatience she did show, but nothing like so much as I quickly began to feel. Then, abruptly, the questions became personal.

"Are you an only child?"

"No. I have an elder sister, married to Mr. Percy Campbell."

Somehow I thought McNab started on hearing this, and after a perceptible pause he added:

"Then you are Miss Cardew now?"

"No; at least I'm not called that. My aunt, who keeps house, is called Miss Cardew, while I am still known as Miss Ann."

"Well, Miss Ann, what friends about your own age have you got, near at hand, to talk to?"

"No one near Redcotes at all."

"That makes it lonely for you. I know myself how great empty spaces, and the silences, stir the imagination."

"On the Marsh it can be very creepy at night," she admitted.

McNab nodded.

"Where there are few people on a wide expanse of country one's imagination begins to fill up the vacancies with an invisible population. In my own country, Miss Ann, among the lonely hills they still believe in witches, warlocks, fairies and water-kelpies." He laughed reminiscently. "I myself was once driven in an ancient dogcart across Skye, from Skaebost to Dunvegan, by an old fellow in a blue jersey and bowler hat who pointed out a place we passed where he had seen a fairy blowing kisses to him."

"But that was all imagination," she said with innocent seriousness.

"Of course," he agreed. "Yet the curious fact is that, when you live in such places, you find it almost easy to believe in such beings."

Ann Cardew turned her eyes full on him, the fleeting smile his anecdote had brought to her lips vanishing, as she became aware of what he was suggesting.

"I see what you mean now," she said slowly.

"You mean that – that what I wrote to you about is like that."

"After Paris," he went on, "life on Romney Marsh must have stirred the imagination of the most prosaic."

I saw her hands clench. She half rose.

"No, no!" she almost sobbed. "No, no, *no!* At any rate it isn't *I* who imagine; it is Father, and he has always lived there. And it isn't anything silly, like ghosts or fairies, it's something terrible and real, quite, quite real, that frightens him."

If he had intended to get behind her self-control he had succeeded. In her protest there was a passion that bordered on hysteria. McNab bent over her, patting her shoulder.

"Very well, Miss Ann," he said gently. "I am going to look into this affair. You have convinced me, at least, that your father's fear is quite real."

The effect was instant. Lifting her head from her hands, she revealed a face almost transfigured with joy.

"And you are sure, now, that it is not all my imagination?" she cried.

"Quite sure," he nodded.

A great sigh of relief and content came. It was a comfort to hear that big, whole-hearted, youthful sigh. She had not observed how little McNab had committed himself. It was one thing for him to say her father's fear was real, and quite another thing to say that her guess at the cause of that fear was correct. But at least he had undertaken to look further into the affair. And this he began to do at once.

"Miss Cardew," he said, "you say in your letter you found your father greatly changed when you came back from Paris, changed both in appearance and disposition. Did anyone who knew him remark on that change?"

"Oh, yes. Several times I've overheard people say Mr. Cardew was growing old very quickly, or something like that."

"That was because of his appearance?"

"Yes, and his change of manner. He – he – gets angry very easily now."

"Can you give me an example? I mean, can you recall some particular incident?"

The girl thought for a moment.

"Well, we have a cowman, George Jippling, who used to be a favourite of Father's. He has always been at Redcotes, and Father trusted him most. The other men were rather jealous of him, but Father never would hear a word against George. But the other day I came into the paddock and heard Father scolding old George before all the men, threatening him with discharge. The poor old man was almost in tears, and when I went to see him in the yard later all he said was: 'Don't yur a-worry yourself, miss. Some of us men do get a bit crotchety-like when we see ourselves get old all of a sudden. But I won't forget how good a master he used to be, that I won't.'"

McNab nodded.

"And have you spoken of this change to anyone?"

"Yes, to Mr. Cyril Campbell."

Again I caught that curious tightening of McNab's lips.

"A neighbour?" he asked.

"My sister Vera is married to his brother Percy. They live at Windygate. I spoke to Cyril because he is a doctor."

"But not the family doctor?"

"Oh, no; that is Dr. Jones, from Appledore. Cyril used to be a medical officer in India, but his health broke down, and when he came home he came to stay with his brother for a time at Windygate."

"And what did he say?"

"Well, he didn't know Father long enough to be so aware of the change. But when I told him I was sure Father went in fear of something he asked a lot of questions, just like a doctor, you know, and said it was probably nothing very serious, but he would speak to Dr. Jones about it. Then when I mentioned how Father watched through the staircase window, as if for someone—"

"One moment," McNab interposed. "What does one see when looking from that window?"

"All the front lawn and the garden."

"And anyone approaching the house?"

"Yes; but it would be difficult at night, for there are trees near the wall, close to the drive, which divides at the gates and then comes up to the front door, where the two drives meet."

"A circular drive, in fact, running along each side of the lawn?"

"Yes, something like that."

"Well, what did Dr. Campbell say when you told him of seeing Mr. Cardew watching through the window?"

Miss Cardew hesitated.

"He asked why I was sure he was not merely resting for a moment. He said it was exactly what he himself sometimes did."

"And what did you say to that?"

Miss Cardew's hands, lying on her lap, clenched slightly.

"I told him he was stupid, and that, whatever he did, Father certainly was looking out as if expecting someone to come, or something to happen."

"You were very sure of that?"

"Oh, yes."

"Well, now, apart from his attitude at the window, had you any other cause for that certainty?"

"I simply felt sure of it."

"You had an – intuition of it?"

"Yes, that's it," Ann Cardew agreed eagerly, "an intuition."

Here I began to tremble for her, for well did I know how McNab scoffed at people who arrived at conclusions through what they called intuition.

"A feminine intuition, in fact?" he added.

And, hearing him, I felt sure we should soon see the last of Miss Ann Cardew and her affairs.

"I suppose so," she agreed now, vaguely aware that something had gone wrong. It had; or both of them would have known that an intuition formed by a woman must necessarily be a feminine intuition. But to McNab, with his passion for logical reasoning, all intuition, whether felt by man or woman, was essentially feminine.

He rose. He got on his feet, that is, in the way I knew well when about to decline a case presented to him for consideration. And that the subtle finality in his attitude had conveyed itself to Miss Cardew was evident to me, for, with desperation in her eyes, she made one last effort to retrieve the situation.

"It's not only that I saw him looking through the window for something!" she cried. "My aunt, too, has noticed he's queer. She, too, has seen him looking for something."

"Through the same window at the same time?"

"No – in his shoes."

McNab was startled. So was I.

"What? Did you say in his shoes?"

The girl nodded, adding hastily:

"Yes, looking for something in his shoes. It seemed so mad I didn't want to mention it; but it's true. Aunt Mary told me herself. Every morning, before he puts on his shoes, he knocks them together, and then looks inside each very carefully. And every night, before he puts on his slippers, he does the same."

After that for quite a time nothing was said.

McNab sat down again, in an abstracted fashion, and I could see he soon became lost in thought. In the silence the ticking of the clock became horribly audible, and all the while Ann Cardew's eyes remained fixed on McNab's downbent head.

At last he looked up.

"Did Dr. Jones come to see your father after you had spoken to Dr. Campbell?"

"Not yet. But it was only last Monday I spoke to Cyril."

"Well, Miss Cardew, I want you to do two things before we go any further. First, go home and arrange at once for Dr. Jones to see your father; then let me know immediately what he says about him." He held up a hand as the girl seemed about to protest. "And at the same time keep on with your own observation of him, and let me know anything else that may happen that strikes you as peculiar."

With that she had to be content. But she went away reluctantly, in a disappointment which was proportionate to the great hopes with which she had come. McNab himself was touched. As soon as the door closed on her he shook his head.

"It's fairly obvious, isn't it? First looking through the staircase window, then looking into his boots, for something that terrorises him. The trouble is not, as you first supposed, cardiac, but cerebral."

"You think it's mental trouble – insanity?"

"Yes. Of course I could not tell her so here and now. But the doctor will see what's wrong. Poor little girl!"

Then that infernal, slow tick, tick of the clock sounded once more; and it was only to break the silence in which it became so distinct and solemn that I spoke.

"McNab, I'm not so sure that there isn't something sinister behind this story. What I mean is, the man may have been terrorised into his present condition. I have a conviction the girl is right."

He looked up; his fingers stopped drumming on his knee.

"But why? When you thought her old you were equally convinced she was wrong. When you find her young and pretty you are convinced she is right."

I ignored the gibe.

"Perhaps you'll tell me how you knew she was young before seeing her. You fooled me enough there. Was it a guess, or an intuition?"

"It was an inference, based on several things in those two letters. You happen to be insensitive to such things, that is all."

"Really? But if you were patient with me, and explained, say, just one thing I missed which revealed her immaturity?"

The humility, I own, was feigned; for, having myself read those letters carefully, I did suspect he had himself merely guessed her youth.

"There is one trivial but almost decisive indication of youth in the first letter which you, as a writer of sorts, ought not to have missed. It comes where she tells of speaking to Cardew about his health, and she adds: 'After that he tried to brighten up and be more like he used to be.' That use of 'like' as a conjunction, common enough now, was confined to kitchen conversation before the war. The 'alright in the morning' is another proof of a post-war education. They rapped knuckles for that sort of thing in the old days," he said, reaching up to the mantelpiece for his pipe. Then he added, half to himself; "Poor wee lass, I doubt there's worse than that coming to her soon."

Worse did come soon. But it came, not in the form Francis McNab expected, but exactly as Ann Cardew seems to have feared it would come. On the next day, Thursday, I happened to be at the tape machine which was ticking out news items from the various news agencies, when a heading caught my eye:

SUDDEN DEATH OF FORMER KENT CRICKETER

Mr. James Cardew, the former well-known Kent batsman, last night dropped dead on the lawn in front of his residence near New Romney. It is presumed the deceased must have felt indisposed previously, for he fell in the middle of the lawn, which, though heavily top-dressed with soil, afforded a quicker approach to the front door than the circular drive. Mr. Cardew, who was 58, took a keen interest in pedigree stock and frequently acted as judge at the various Agricultural Society shows. Several circumstances associated

> with the occurrence have decided the authorities
> to hold an inquest, the date of which has not yet
> been fixed.

When the news editor had boiled this down to the four lines he thought it worth to a London daily, I took the tape machine slip round to McNab.

He showed no trace of emotion till he came to the last sentence. Then I noticed that the flimsy slip of paper fluttered slightly in his hand.

"It has come once again to look like heart trouble," I remarked.

He nodded abstractedly.

"If it's foul play, you could have done nothing, McNab."

"Nothing to stop it," he said. "I wonder if she got home before it happelied. No." he added, "I could have done nothing in the time. She came too late, and she knew too little."

Still, I could see from his manner that he was not pleased with himself, that he did not altogether exonerate himself; and from this I knew his mind now harboured a suspicion of the possibility of foul play.

"I think," he said at length, "I'd like you to go down for the inquest."

"Me?" I said, astonished.

"Yes. Your holiday begins tomorrow, and I've a job on hand – a minor affair, but I can't drop it now. Find out what are the circumstances which call for an inquest. If anything suspicious emerges, wire me at once."

Chapter 3

On Ashford railway platform next morning, while the New Romney train was being backed into the station, I told myself that attendance at an inquest was, of all, the most unlikely holiday a journalist would choose. And yet, though it had been chosen for me, I knew, as the train jogged on towards the Marsh, I would not have it otherwise. This was certainly not like going out on duty. I had no notebook or pencils in my pocket; but I had a sense of being free.

As soon, however, as the train left the fair, smiling wooded lands and comfortable looking houses of the Weald behind and dropped down to the Marsh, the abrupt change in the aspect of the country at once attracted my attention. Now there was little for the eye to rest on except a vast, green level expanse, intersected by long stretches of narrow dykes full of black, stagnant water. Across many little bridges spanning the dykes the train passed, with a momentary reverberation like the rumble of drums.

Only here and there, at long intervals, could one perceive any signs of an active human life; but now and then, in the distance, one caught sight of a church spire on some little eminence, around which a few trees seemed to huddle together. The impression it all made on me was curious. I looked up from where I sat to see if the sky had become overcast with clouds. But no, it was not that. And the sense of chill I experienced could not come from an approach to the sea, for we were yet some way from New Romney, and, though the little town had once been a seaport, I was aware that long ago the sea had retreated and left New Romney over a mile inland.

But, as I puzzled over the sombre impression this marsh country made on me, something McNab had said to Ann Cardew came back – something about the way in which men are made credulous, and the human spirit is affected, made to feel small and insignificant, by living among mountains. And I asked myself then if a great, monotonous, level expanse of empty country could have a similar dwarfing effect. I had not settled the question before the train pulled up at New Romney.

At the local police station I interviewed the sergeant with an increased sense of responsibility. Not so improbable now did Miss Cardew's fears seem. When humanity is made to look, on such a background, so unimportant, when such loneliness would make murder seem both easy and safe, murder there might well have been.

So, at least, I had come to feel when I put my question about the inquest to the station-sergeant. The office was small and stuffy. Against the shut window a strayed bumble bee buzzed noisily, searching for an exit. Under the window a constable, tunic unbuttoned, sat before a table, busy with a ledger.

"Twelve tomorrow," said the sergeant, "in the schoolroom at Burrish."

"How far?"

"Three miles."

"Any inn there where I could put up for the night?"

The burly sergeant glanced me over.

"There's the Woolpack; but you'd do better at the New Inn here."

"I'll risk the Woolpack."

"A bus will leave here in time for the inquest tomorrow."

The impression came that he did not want me at Burrish then.

"By the way, sergeant, I suppose you know what the circumstances are which have necessitated an inquest?" I said.

The young constable at the desk looked up, and the two men exchanged a swift glance before the sergeant eyed me again.

"I suppose I do," he said. "What of it?"

"Well, what of it?" I echoed.

"You'll no doubt hear all about that tomorrow, at the inquest," said he.

That he did not mean to tell me what the circumstances were now became obvious. This secrecy was unusual. Unless there is something very exceptional indeed in the circumstances that call for an inquest, the police are not uncommunicative to newspaper men. Then I remembered I had not told him I was a journalist. I had been trying to forget the fact myself, and it rather pleased me to perceive from his reticence that the sergeant had not suspected my occupation. I said casually:

"Well, there seems to be a rumour that there's more in this man's death than shows on the surface."

The sergeant affected surprise, stopped fingering his moustache to gaze at me. Then he shook his head.

"That rumour hasn't reached us," he said.

"And I'm afraid, I'm very much afraid, that if your paper has sent you from London on account of it you're in for a disappointment."

So he had detected me! I wondered what gave me away. It nettled me to know it must be something fairly obvious for a country police sergeant to detect me so easily. This conclusion, however, did less than justice to the country policeman in general, and Sergeant Strood in particular. But this I had yet to learn. And so, perceiving the hint of a smile gather round the young policeman's mouth as he bent over his ledger, and seeing the sergeant fingering away at his moustache so complacently, I was tempted to startle him out of his self-contented assurance. With feigned reluctance I turned away.

"Sorry if there's to be no story for my paper in this," I remarked casually. "That means, I take it, you have failed to discover what was in the dead man's shoes."

The twinkle vanished from the sergeant's eye: the young policeman threw up his head sharply. Even the big bumble bee seemed to be stunned into a momentary silence by his vain efforts to take a header through the glass. And for a time both the men seemed equally paralysed. The sergeant was the first to recover.

"We know what was in his shoes," he nodded meaningly.

It was my turn to be startled.

"What was it?" I cried, unable to restrain my excitement.

"His feet," said the sergeant. "I give you my word for it. You may safely send that fact to your paper, and say you have it on the authority of Sergeant Strood."

But I could afford to let the sergeant have his pleasantry at my expense. I had learned quite as much as I expected to learn.

At the New Inn I made a good lunch, though I didn't dally over it. For it was now clear the police had their suspicions of something unusual behind the death of Mr. Cardew. They knew something, and possibly suspected more. But as I made my way out of New Romney and took the road towards Burrish the thought came that I would give much to know on what their suspicion, if any, was founded. Had Ann Cardew been to see Sergeant Strood, or had the police arrived at some conclusion of their own, independently? Of course, if any uneasiness the police might have about the death was derived exclusively from Miss Ann Cardew, there still might be nothing in it – nothing, that is, beyond what we had already heard from her; and that alone would not warrant me in sending off that wire to McNab. What McNab had said was that if anything suspicious emerged I was to send a wire, and I took it now that it must be something independent of, and in addition to, anything Miss Cardew had said. That was what I had to discover as soon as possible. And since Strood would not talk – might not, indeed, divulge all he knew even at tomorrow's inquest – my best chance was to get among the people on the spot with the least possible delay.

Perhaps it was this pressing anxiety on my part that made the miles to Burrish seem so long. Possibly it was the nature of the Marsh road. For a time one was walking along a straight road, flanked by deep dykes full of water one couldn't see because of the tall thick reeds growing on the slopes of the dykes. And then there would come a sharp, right-angle turn, with another turn to the left further on that almost appeared to be taking me back the way I had come. And, as I afterwards found, all Marsh roads were like that. Nasty roads to drive, or even to walk on, in the dark, I thought they would be. There was the long straight section to lull one into a sense of security, then the sudden right or left twist, with, for the incautious, a sudden plunge through the rustling reeds down the slope, followed by a splash in the waters. And Heaven help you if you couldn't extricate yourself, I thought, pausing on one of the small bridges to look down on the jet-black water.

In the night few could be on these roads. Even that afternoon I had not seen a soul since turning inland off the one main road that traverses the Marsh, mostly by the seashore, from Hythe, in Kent, to Rye, in Sussex. Once or twice, far ahead of me, I saw what seemed to be someone standing by the roadside, watching something in the dyke below; but, on approaching, the thing turned out to be a gaunt dwarf tree, so ancient as to be almost leafless, its bleak gnarled and twisted stem bearing witness to the riot of winds which, in their season, swept that great expanse.

By this time I should have been glad to meet anyone, if only to ascertain in what direction Burrish lay. Of this I was now by no means sure, for I had twice come on crossroads, and, although each had its rickety direction post, the place names had long ago been weathered out of existence, and it was clear that into that hinterland of the Marsh few travelled except natives, who needed no guidance.

But a little later I discovered that the road was not so deserted as it looked.

Having just turned another of those endless corners – this one screened by a clump of thorn bushes and two or three dwarf hornbeams – I opened out a new stretch of road breaking away to the right. At the far end of this stretch, about a mile away, I saw a few white houses, and behind them, on a slight eminence, a church spire, encircled by trees. The unexpected sight made me pause.

The road itself, running straight between the parallel dykes, with the tall reeds growing up to its very edge on both sides, was as empty as ever. But I did not mind now: if this were not Burrish itself, at least there were houses at which I could obtain directions. I was just about to push on again when I saw something ahead which kept me motionless. Unwittingly I had paused close to the dark thorn bushes, and in the shadow they cast on the road I must have been very hard to see. Anyhow, the man who thrust his head and shoulders out of the reeds about three hundred yards along the road did not seem to observe me.

He himself, however, was startlingly distinct to me, for against that white road, and in that alley of light green reeds, his dark blue uniform – even the little of it that was visible – made a contrast that could not be missed. What was the policeman watching? I soon saw it must be something between me and himself, for I could see his observation did not travel as far along the road as the corner where I stood.

When my eyes, from trying to see what or who was being watched, went back to the watcher himself, I got a shock: it was Sergeant Strood! He ducked out of sight again; but I had not long to wait. The first glance when the head came up once more left me in no doubt. The rubicund face, which amid the sea of swaying reeds made him seem like a swimmer in distress, was that of the sergeant. But how had he got there ahead of me? And was it for me he watched? Was he going to stop me from getting to Burrish?

I recalled the impression I had taken while in the office talking to him: that he was not quite willing to see me go to Burrish, that day at least. Had he now found a better pretence for stopping me than that the New Inn at New Romney was more comfortable than the Woolpack? That got me on the move again. But the sergeant was quick to see me now: I had not taken three brisk steps forward before he sank out of sight abruptly, as if pulled from below.

With redoubled curiosity I kept on up the road, meaning to fish him out of his cover, and to that end keeping my eyes fixed on the spot where he had ducked. That I might spoil whatever job he was on did not trouble me, for he, on his part, had not been very helpful to me. And it did not cross my mind that anything very serious could lie behind this Jack-in-the-box hide-and-seek business.

But, some fifty yards on, the tail of my watchful eye took in something on the other side of the road. Looking round, I saw a gap in the reeds, opening on to a small stone bridge over the dyke, and on the bridge a gate which gave access to the field beyond. Sitting with his back to the gate was a man who, cigarette in mouth, appeared to be busy doing some repair to a motorcycle. The brief glance he shot at me was enough to let me see he was a dark-eyed, sharp-featured, clean-shaven man in the early thirties. He did not seem in the best of humour.

"Could you tell me," I asked, pulling up, "if that is Burrish I see ahead?"

"It is," he replied, without again looking up.

He received my thanks with a nod.

"Puncture?" I asked affably, drawing a little nearer.

To this he deigned no reply at all. But none was needed. I could see the puncture for myself. And he was having trouble with it, not only because it was not more than an inch from the valve socket, but also because it was in the back wheel tyre. It is curious to remember just what this was to mean later on. He did not seem very expert. I took another step nearer.

"Can I help?"

"No, thanks."

The tone of voice would have been enough without the look. He looked daggers, as it used to be called, at me. I certainly had ample time to fix his face in my memory before he began to stuff the red tube back inside its cover.

"Well, good day," I remarked, that being what I understood they always say in the country. He said nothing.

I went on towards the spot where Sergeant Strood lay hidden. Perhaps he would have more to say this time. But it would not be so easy to find him now that I had taken my eyes off the spot where he had disappeared. Along the whole length of that road there was so little variation in the road itself, or in the immense bulrushes covering the dyke slopes, that one yard of it did not seem to differ by a hair from any other.

I determined to root him out, however; and, if this did spoil his business with the other man, I owed him one for his treatment of me. Besides, it would be as well, if the Cardew affair turned out to be serious, to let this rural policeman see at once that I, too, could play the obstructive game. Strood was even harder to find than I expected. After hunting up and down twice or thrice I began to think he must have got away along the bottom of the dyke while I was speaking with the other man. But our interchange of words had been too brief for that; and of course I must have seen, from where I stood, those heavy sedges swaying had he tried to creep through them. Still, he might well have wriggled some little way from where I had last seen him.

Then, just when I caught sight of something, the sudden loud detonations of a motor engine burst on my ear, and I turned to see my amiable motorcyclist out on the road running beside his bike. With a hop and a skip he was in the saddle and away like an arrow. I turned round to look at the pair of shoes I had seen a yard or two in among the bulrushes. My spirits had been rising ever since I had come out of the loneliness of the Marsh and into touch again with humanity.

It is queer how merely to see a fellow creature in an undignified position gives us a sense of superiority over him. The man we see chasing the hat bumping and rolling in the gutter may be a great statesman or a great poet, yet while the undignified pursuit lasts the amusement he rouses makes us feel his superior. And the sergeant's position was more than undignified. I remembered his lofty manner with me at the police station, and laughed aloud.

"I know what's in these shoes, anyhow," I said very meaningly. "A pair of feet. Sergeant Strood's, I think."

The sergeant, after a pause, drew his feet up, got on his knees and rose. But he did not look in the least sheepish as he waded out to join me on the road.

"I could arrest you for this, you know," he said with a curt nod.

"Arrest me? On what charge?" I demanded.

"Obstructing the police in the execution of their duty."

"How could I be obstructing you? Why, you weren't even on the road. Even if I'd told the man you were there that wouldn't constitute obstruction."

Strood, in the act of flicking his knees with a red bandana handkerchief, paused.

"Do you think he knew I was there?"

"How can I say? He knew something that spoiled his temper, anyhow."

Strood grinned.

"That would do it, if he knew! But I hope he didn't."

"What's he been up to – exceeding the speed limit?"

"Well, you might call it that," Strood replied in a way that showed me that, given fuller information, I might with more exactness call it something else.

"You must have exceeded the speed limit yourself to get here ahead of me," I said.

The sergeant smiled knowingly.

"But even so," I went on, "you must have passed me on the road without being seen. How was that done?"

"There's a path across the fields."

"Oh, you didn't tell me that," I said, thinking that for reticence there was nothing to beat a rural policeman.

Strood shook his head. "No good to you. You'd never have found the planks across all the dykes. Most Marsh villages have these footways to them. In the old days the smugglers made them to keep clear of the roads, and so. But I cut him short. Though he looked willing enough to talk on ancient law-breakers, it was the contemporary ones I wanted to get at.

"In the present day the only crime you have is, I suppose, sheep-stealing."

Strood stared at me.

"There's nothing here to steal except sheep," I declared. "No doubt that really is what made you watch that young fellow at the gate there."

Such ignorance of country life obviously amazed the sergeant. For a second I saw in his eye a desire to enlighten this ignorant town dweller. But he checked his instructive impulses.

"Well, you might call it that too – sheep stealing. And a damn silly sheep at that," he added, below his breath, as he bent again to complete his work with the red handkerchief.

His last words brought the sudden thought that this might, after all, have some connection with the Cardew affair. Strood's manner was portentous; it was that of the man with inside information who is talking with an outsider. My experience had taught me that in such a situation the best attitude to adopt was that of one completely ignorant and innocent; for then the other's vanity is usually unable to resist a display of his superior knowledge. This method, I had found, occasionally worked even with McNab.

"He had no sheep with him this time," I said.

Strood sniffed significantly.

"Did you expect to see it riding pillion on the bike?" he inquired.

"Now you're laughing at me, sergeant," I protested.

"Am I?" Strood drew closer and, tapping my chest with his forefinger, whispered: "What if he left her hid in them rushes same as I was?"

"Let's go and look," I whispered back. "You yourself weren't hard to find."

He followed me along the road till we reached the gap that led through the gate into the pastures beyond. But I found nothing after a careful inspection on both sides of the place where the young man had sat.

"You must have been mistaken," I said to Strood. "There's nothing here – nothing living, anyway, as far as I can see."

Strood, who had been leaning with his arms on the top rail of the gate, inspecting the field, turned to me.

"I don't know how far you can see," he remarked dryly, "but to my eye now" – he indicated the distant end of the field – "there's something very much alive over there."

Following the direction given by his pointing finger I saw a woman running, running like a deer, away from us, and bending low as she ran. But she was not quick enough. I had seen her before – once before. It was Ann Cardew!

Chapter 4

The sight of Ann Cardew there left me dumb – dumb, and a trifle breathless. For one thing, it was unexpected to find that this almost ludicrous incident with Strood and the motorcyclist might well have some connection with the matter which had brought me there; for another, it was startling to find that Ann Cardew, the very person who had called us in, was herself being watched by the police. I was forced, then, to do some swift thinking while Strood, thin-lipped and frowning, kept his eyes narrowed on the running girl.

Strood had, of course, all along known she was there. Plainly his object had been to overhear what passed between Ann Cardew and the man; and then I had blundered in and spoilt his game. The fact that he had lingered afterwards to talk with me proved that he had no need to identify the girl. He knew who she was already. But what the sergeant could not know was that I, too, knew who she was. Possibly I could use this knowledge to make him tell me more. But, not at the moment seeing how to do this, my thoughts took another turn.

The significance of Sergeant Strood's presence there arrested me. A meeting between a young man and a girl in a country lane does not usually interest the police. Yet this meeting immensely interested Strood. If the police really did hold some suspicions of their own that Cardew had been murdered, then I might as well send for McNab that night.

But, just as I was beginning to glow at the speed with which I had fulfilled the mission on which McNab had sent me, a flood of questions pulled me up: had Ann Cardew spoken to the local police of her suspicions, and had this motorcyclist come under their suspicion, and was she, acting by their instructions in meeting this man? The flush of self-satisfaction ebbed away. If Ann Cardew alone had raised police suspicion by telling them the same tale as she had told us, I was no further forward than before I came.

But when I recalled Strood's talk of sheep-stealing, and, above all, his reference to this particular sheep's intelligence, I saw that could not be the position. Whatever suspicions the police held they could not be derived from Ann Cardew. Otherwise Strood would not have referred to her in the terms he had used.

Then, in a flash, the situation cleared as I saw what lay before me: I had to find out from Strood just what had aroused suspicion or doubt in the minds of the local authorities.

It was at this point that the girl reached the fence, the sergeant's sharp eyes still upon her. A plan of action came to me. I sprang it on him.

"You think her father was murdered?" I whispered in his ear.

Strood almost jumped. I certainly had amazed him.

"What – what's that you say?" he stammered.

Then he added, "You know her, then?"

"We know more than you would ever guess, down here."

He drew a breath or two.

"Somebody's been talking, eh?"

"A queer story came our way. You'll be able to read it in Monday's *Record*."

"Is that your paper?"

"It's the paper I'm on. I came here to investigate the story. So far all I've got in support is the picturesque incident of you hiding in these rushes, and my having to pull you out."

Horror shot over his face.

"You wouldn't put that in?" he gasped.

"Why not? Now I think of it, it will make an excellent heading for the whole article:

"Why was the Sergeant Hidden in the Bulrushes?"

Strood's countenance turned to a deeper ruby. He thrust out a despairing hand.

"My God!" he whispered hoarsely. "I might be laughed out of Kent."

This was the point at which, to leave his imagination time to hear the laughter, I took out and lit a cigarette. He, too, was silent for a space.

"Did you know, sir," he said at length, "that my first name is Matthew?"

"No – what of it?" I asked in surprise.

"Only this," he replied nervously. "Only this: if you print that about me being hidden in the bulrushes they'll start calling me Moses right away. I know 'em! Sergeant Matt they call me now, but Sergeant Moses I'll be known as to the end of my days."

"You don't like being laughed at?"

Strood shook his head.

"It don't do, sir, for an officer to get himself made a laughing stock in his district. Our superiors don't like it, and believe me, sir, they don't forget it neither."

This was the moment for me to strike.

"Well, sergeant, it's quite simple," I said. "If you don't want to see yourself figuring in the *Record* under the caption; Why was the Sergeant Hidden in the Bulrushes? there's only one thing to do."

He was too agitated to notice the cigarette I offered him.

"What's that?"

"Just tell me now why you were hiding in them."

His face fell again,

"Can't be done."

"Have you had instructions to say nothing?"

"N – o, not exactly; but we've to keep mum pending investigation. We don't want any publicity yet."

"Then you're going the right way to get what you don't want. The case will have full publicity on Monday. Make no mistake about that – full publicity – and you too," I added.

"Do you mean that if I *did* tell you you wouldn't print anything?"

"Of course; that's exactly what I offered. We're always anxious to work hand in hand with the police, and if any newspaper publishes anything that hinders you in a case it's simply because some stupid officer has kept us in the dark as to the inward significance of some apparently harmless item of news that reaches us. But mutual confidence there must be. You can't gag the Press – not in England, anyhow."

He was a hard nut to crack, that sergeant. Even then he wavered and hesitated. But I had too tight a squeeze on him. Presently, after some heavy thinking, he was able to recognise which was the lesser of two evils. Even then, though, he needed something more to make him speak. By good luck that something more came along in the nick of time. As I stood waiting I heard the rumble of wheels on the road. Then a dog-cart with two men in it hove into sight and the driver, on catching sight of us, pulled up with a jerk. He was a very stout old man with a cheery, rosy face.

"Goo' day, sergeant," he hailed.

"Good day, Mr. Holley," Strood returned formally.

"Sad business this about Mr. Cardew," the driver remarked, making use of the halt to get out his matches to light his pipe.

Strood agreed, while he exchanged greetings with the other man, who was small, with nervously bright eyes, though pink-complectioned also, and, like the other, obviously of the farmer class.

"Be it true as the crowner ain't a-settin' with a jury?" he piped as he eyed me.

"That's so, Mr. Uden. Nothing in the case to call for a jury," Strood replied.

The small man's bird-like eyes fluttered back to the sergeant.

"We were talking about it as we came along," he remarked.

"Yes?"

"Everybody do be talking around Burrish," Holley added, heaving sideways to replace his matchbox. "It's been in the newspapers, I've heard."

Strood said nothing.

"There's nothing like the newspapers to set folks talking," Uden remarked.

It was a most helpful remark, and I lost my impatience to see the dog-cart move on again.

"Ah, well, 'twere a sudden call," Holley nodded.

"Hard to believe I was talking to him last Tuesday in Ashford. That's what I said to Uden here, as we passed the churchyard, and saw old Zacchary a-digging of his grave. A sudden call – isn't that what I said, George?"

"You did, Holley, you did. A sudden call is what I heard you call it. And I've heard some folks say it may have been an over-sudden call."

"I wouldn't say that exactly," Holley remarked judicially. "He hasn't been looking very grand for a long time. Still, it were a sudden call, when all's said and done."

For a time they moralised rather lugubriously over life and mortality in the manner of country folk. At last Holley gave a flick to the flank of the shaggy horse, and the ancient dog-cart rumbled off.

As soon as they were out of sight Sergeant Strood leant back against the gate, his arms stretched along the top rail. The relaxed attitude somehow betokened surrender. I was now aware that I was about to hear all he knew of the case.

"It's Hackett I've got to thank for this," he said. "Hackett and Jippling between them"

"Yes," I said encouragingly.

"Hackett and Jippling between them will have made the police force the laughing-stock of the country, if I can't stop it."

"One moment before you go on; who are they?"

"They're the two who got this inquest to be held: George Jippling who found the body, and Hackett who said and did things before Jippling which started him gossiping. But it's not Jippling I blame for all the gossip, it's Hackett."

"And who is Hackett?"

"Hackett is the young constable you saw in the office. A little too smart Hackett is at times. Hackett cherishes fancies about quick promotion, and becoming a famous detective." Strood cleared his throat and wheeled round to expectorate.

"No actual harm in that, of course, but I do get a bit fed up at having to listen to his fancy talk."

"Go on," I urged.

"Well, it happened like this. When Jippling found the body lying on the lawn he goes to the house to break the news, and old Miss Cardew rings up Windygate, to call Dr. Campbell, whose brother was Mr. Cardew's son-in-law, as he could come quicker than Dr. Jones from Appledore. Both the Mr. Campbells were away in London, but Hackett was at Windygate, in the house, at the time, courting the parlourmaid of course; and he, getting the news from the girl, phones up Dr. Jones, and then cycles over to Redcotes. That's how the trouble began. While they're waiting for Dr. Jones, Jippling tells Hackett how he'd seen Mr. Cardew coming along the road when something queer happened. He saw Mr. Cardew pull up short, and then bend down and look at his feet."

"At his feet!" I echoed involuntarily. Strood smiled wanly.

"At his *shoes*, if you like it better – shoes or feet, they were close enough together. But after I've done you'll find it was at neither he was really looking. Well, as I was saying, Jippling says, in the statement Hackett took from him, that he heard Mr. Cardew, as he bent, utter a sudden startled cry, and then straighten himself, and after a stagger or two come quickly along the road, pass through his own gate and up on to the lawn, where he fell dead. This, of course, was just the sort of story to set Hackett's fancies a-fire, and off he goes, without waiting for the doctor to arrive, to search the road. Naturally he found nobody – there wouldn't be by that time, anyway. But there never had been, Jippling swears."

"So he found nothing?" I said.

"He found an empty silver cigarette case lying in the centre of the road, exactly thirty yards five inches from the spot where Jippling stood at his gate looking on. That was the first thing he found. The other thing was a short stick, standing on the grass by the side of the road, just opposite where he picked up the cigarette case."

"Go on, sergeant."

"It was just the sort of stick a child would shove into the turf with a piece of paper for a flag. As for the cigarette case, we found who it belonged to at once. And there, to Hackett's disappointment, the thing might have ended, since Dr. Jones, after further examination, was ready to give his certificate of death from heart failure – might have ended, I was saying, but for two queer facts which we can't so far understand. The first is: why didn't Mr. Cardew pick up the cigarette case when he saw it lying on the ground; and the second is: why did the owner of the case deny it was his when it was shown to him?"

"That is certainly odd," I assented.

Strood nodded agreement.

"That's what I think, though of course the person who identified the cigarette case may be mistaken."

"It had no initials on it?"

"No, but it's a good article, of plain, solid silver. Hackett's, of course, all for keeping it safe to get fingerprints off it. It's all Hackett's doing, of course – all the gossip, I mean. Comes of being so young, and full of zeal, as they call it. Precious near getting us all laughed at, he is, what with raising false hopes in the public's mind of a murder case, and starting all the gossip that's brought you down here to write about it." Sergeant Strood sighed gently, straightened himself, and readjusted his peaked cap.

It must be owned I was disappointed. Not yet had I obtained a sufficient justification for bringing McNab down. The one item of possible significance now left was the unclaimed cigarette case.

Strood, getting ready to depart, cut into my thoughts.

"Well, anyway, that's the whole story," he said with formality.

Then I remembered.

"Not the whole story, sergeant. You haven't yet told me why you were hiding in the bulrushes."

The sergeant looked pained.

"You won't say that action had no connection with this affair?" I challenged him.

"Well, it had and it hadn't. You see, that motorcyclist, Mr. Sneyd, is the supposed owner of the cigarette case, and it was Miss Cardew – Miss Ann, that is – who identified it as Mr. Sneyd's. And so, seeing them together, I took the chance of – well, just hearing what passed between them."

"And I spoiled that?"

"You did. But, so long as you print nothing about that, I don't think there's, so far, any harm done. And of course I've got your word on that," he added.

What surprised me was the straight, intent look which accompanied his words. Wondering what that look meant, I watched him till, a little way along the road, he stepped in among the waving rushes to cross the dyke by some unknown means and take some path invisible to me. For all that it seemed so flat and open the Marsh afforded excellent cover.

After vainly watching a while to see if I could again pick up the sergeant's broad blue back anywhere, I turned towards Burrish. And the thought that went with me was that the Cardew drama would prove in the end to be rather like the Marsh itself – an affair in which much lay hidden beneath an apparent surface simplicity. There was in it, I suspected, more – much more – than met the eye. So at least I interpreted Sergeant Strood's last, warning look.

I had not long to wait before this suspicion crystallised into a certainty.

Chapter 5

The Woolpack, as a closer approach revealed, stood at the junction of four roads. It was a long, two-storey house with the dark wooden framing of the Tudor period, a high-pitched roof of weather-worn, mossy red tiles, and, whether real or sham Tudor, looked a bright and pleasant hostelry. Except for an old man seated on a bench against the house, with a tankard and an old bowler hat on the table in front of him, no one seemed to be about; but the front door stood open, and I made for it across the rather wide space which separated the house from the road. The old fellow surveyed me keenly over the top of his tankard.

"Very hot," I remarked.

"Ay, so it be for the time of year. Come far?" he inquired.

"New Romney. Hardly met a soul on the road, But of course the Marsh is thinly populated."

"Nowadays." Then with much complacency he said: "It's me as has put most of them away."

I had been glancing about for a bell or knocker to attract attention. Somewhere in the back the murmur of voices could be heard. But his last surprising remark drew my attention back to the man. He was most shabbily clothed, and old, but his eyes made one doubt if he were as old as the long pointed grey beard made him appear, for those eyes had still both colour and lustre. An odd-looking fellow. The top of his bald head was quite flat, with no back to it, and this, with the long pointed beard and the bead-like eyes, made him look rather like a human goat. With a nod he repeated his last remark more loudly:

"It's me as has put most of the people away."

"You are the landlord?" I hazarded vaguely.

He cackled shortly.

"'Tain't beer as lays 'em out. Good beer could do it, supposin' they 'ad took enough and tried to walk home wi' the dykes to right and left awaitin' for 'em to totter in. That did use to 'appen in the good old days." He contemplated his tankard sorrowfully. "But the beer what was in this mug afore I finished it" – he shook his head— "that couldn't do it."

"No good?"

"Oh, well, there's no harm in it, of course – leastways, the only 'arm in it is you 'ardly feel you've 'ad any till you've 'ad more than a poor man like me can pay for."

Already I had barked my knuckles on the old oak of the door, and, with no result, had tried a cough or two inside. That the Woolpack would have neither porter nor reception-clerk I could well believe; still, there must be some way of getting attention. The old fellow saw my difficulty.

"You've got to make a noise," he explained, "or they won't 'ear."

"There's nothing to make it with," I returned, rather exasperated, "unless you bang that tankard of yours on the table, if it's empty."

"It's empty all right, mister; but I can't bang it all the same. They'd think I was callin' for another pint."

"Bang it, then," I said.

Promptly and heartily he obeyed.

In response a young man in shirt-sleeves presently appeared. At my request for a room there and then he looked doubtful. They didn't usually have anyone except in the holiday months, but he would find his mother and see if a room could be got ready for the night. Would I be staying for one night only? To this question I hastened to say I would want the room probably for several days, adding, to make it seem better worthwhile, that perhaps later a friend would join me.

He took up my suitcase, and as he was placing it inside the door I asked him to bring me out a glass of the Woolpack beer. A cough from the old man reminded me just in time.

"Perhaps you'll join me, Mr...?"

"Thankee, sir. Moss is the name, Zacchary Moss. For forty-three years sexton to this 'ere parish, is what they'd carve on my monument if I 'ad dropped dead just now."

Then I understood his previous saying about his share in putting away the population. There was a spade against the wall on his further side. He seemed likely to be talkative. I sat down as soon as our beer arrived, and pulled out my pipe.

"Nothing goes better wi' beer than a smoke," Mr. Moss remarked in a wistful tone as he watched me light up. "I'd 'ave one myself if I 'adn't mislaid my baccy last Wensday."

When his pipe was going he looked me over with a critical eye.

"Ain't come 'ere for your 'ealth, 'ave you?" he inquired.

Prepared as I was to let him put his own questions before putting mine, this question, from him, I did not like. Somehow it had a professional touch about it. And there was that spade of his standing against the wall.

"My health?" I echoed. "Certainly not."

"You'll excuse me. We don't see many strangers this way, and I couldn't 'elp wondering what brought you. At first I thought you must be a traveller. I knowed Farmer Holley was thinking about getting a new patent turnip-masher, and I thought you'd be the traveller come to see 'im about it – till I 'eard you was going to stay, which he wouldn't do."

"I'm a writer."

"Meanin' books?"

"Something like that. It's about the Marsh I want to write."

Moss set down his tankard hurriedly to chuckle.

"Dang me if ever I'd a guessed that 'un," he declared. "When I 'eard you ask for a room, and knowed you couldn't be Holley's traveller, dang me again if I didn't take 'ee for a gentleman."

At this point, before I got going with my own questions, the landlady appeared in the doorway. But, when I followed her to see the room she offered, I gave an order for what I thought would be enough beer to keep Moss fixed on his bench till I returned.

Mrs. Beddoes was a pleasant-faced little woman, and, as soon became apparent, a very tidy one. Such old houses as hers may be very picturesque, with their long passages, odd-shaped rooms, open rafters and whitewashed walls, but they must be very hard to keep in good order. The amount of old oak in the staircase, bedrooms and long, dark passages, with a step down here and a step up there, where least expected, this probably reduced the necessary work, for the wood, hardened by time and polished by use, had taken on a surface of its own.

When Mrs. Beddoes flung open the door of the room she proposed to get ready for me, I was surprised at its size. Indeed, the size of the whole place mystified me, till I learned something of the old-time history of the smuggling trade that flourished for centuries in Romney Marsh. The Woolpack, so remotely situated in the centre of the Marsh, had been a great place of resort; and I was shown a long, low, panelled room, next my own, which had served as a sort of council chamber and meeting place for the actual smugglers and their agents and customers from inland parts. But, interesting as all this was, it has no bearing direct or indirect on the Cardew case, and it is perhaps advisable to say at once that the tragedy which was to follow might just as well have played itself out in an ugly modern semi-detached red-brick villa for all that the age or architecture of the house had to do with it. If the Woolpack did have any sliding panels or secret passages, I never discovered where they were, and certainly no one concerned in this narrative ever made any use of them.

But all the time, while I followed behind Mrs. Beddoes as she proudly showed me over the house, I was on edge to resume my gossip with Zacchary Moss. The landlady I could get to gossip at any moment; but Moss, I suspected, talked freely only under the stimulus of much beer.

Finally, having shown me over the ancient house, the good woman, glowing with my words of admiration, stopped by the double window at the top of the narrow staircase to indicate the extensive prospect one had from that position. One certainly saw a long way over that flat country from even so moderate a height, and, seen through the open lattices after wandering over the dark interior, very colourful the Marsh looked on that bright afternoon. Right across the green levels of the dyke-fretted fields the eye travelled unimpeded till one saw the long, straight line of downs, like a deep blue rampart, beyond which stretched the higher level of the Weald. But my gaze quickly returned to the Marsh itself. Its silence and emptiness fascinated me, and the sombre impression I had first received in the train returned. I tried to analyse the cause. It ought to have been a cheerful prospect, and yet, somehow, was not. It was full of colour, and yet, somehow, it had more than a tinge of the sinister about it.

Nothing that moved could be seen on all its wide expanse. Here and there, among its intricate network of dykes, one could see the light touch the water at some bend and turn it into a curve of quicksilver that looked like an attempt at a smile. But it was more like a fixed grin. Nothing moved on its surface – not even the water. It was like a green mask set in a knowing, rather malicious smirk.

"Quiet and peaceful it do look, don't it, sir?" Mrs. Beddoes' voice at my elbow recalled me.

"Y – es." I hesitated. "But it's – too – too still."

"Still?" she repeated, perplexed.

"Well, there's nothing that moves on it – nothing that shows, I mean."

Then she smiled.

"Easy to see you're a town-bred gentleman, sir. If you knew the country you'd see plain enough. Why, even from here I can see my boy Ben among the sheep t'other side of the Borden dyke. But of course," she added consolingly, "on the Ma'sh you've got to know where to look for what you wants to see."

Then she bustled off to get my room ready, leaving me standing at the top of the stairs.

Well, these last words went home in a way she, honest soul, never guessed. *You've got to know where to look for what you want to see – on the Marsh!* I whispered to myself as I descended. That was my trouble! Mighty keen I was to know where to look just then, for there was still time to get McNab down for the inquest next day. Yet I was mortally afraid of putting my foot into it by seeming to be too curious or over-interested. And I knew what damage could be done to a case by even one indiscreet question; how fatally a pitch could be queered, so to speak, before the investigation began. Yet Zacchary Moss seemed safe enough. I remembered Ben had gone off to attend to the sheep, and a glance at my watch showed that it was after three o'clock – past closing time.

I hurried downstairs, doubtful if I could detain Mr. Moss when there was no longer any beer to be had. In the hall the sound of voices from outside pulled me up.

"A nice-spoken young chap he is, and open-handed too," I heard Zacchary declare.

"Well, I saw Sergeant Matt and he wi' their heads together along the Romney road a little while agone."

"You try and get something outen him, Zacchary," another voice urged. "Sergeant Matt mightn't be so tight-lipped wi' a foreigner."

"That's a good notion, now! Just you bring up the name of Cardew, promiscuous like, and say you've been diggin' his—"

"Pah!" a voice cut in, "that's no good. Don't you know that after a little diggin' the only thing Zacchary Moss wants to get out'en anybody is beer?"

A laugh went round. Moss's voice came in indignation:

"I'll promise to ask for no beer after diggin' for you, Thomas Vidler."

"Meaning?"

"Meanin' that to bury some folks gives me enough pleasure in itself!" Moss snapped.

"You'll 'ave to wait for't, then."

"That's as may be. All flesh is grass, Tom Vidler. Sudden death on the Ma'sh bain't so uncommon. Mr. Cardew, 'ee wasn't so old as you, nor did 'ee live so ungodly neither."

At this point a creaking behind made me turn, to see Mrs. Beddoes appear on the stairs. Fortunately the pile of bedclothes she carried prevented her from seeing me at once. But I was forced into the open.

Moss sat where I left him, and of the two who sat on the same bench one was the stout farmer, Holley, whom I had already seen. Uden stood, glass in hand, beside another man. Holley, tossing off the last of his ale, set down the glass and wiped his lips.

"Ah, well, that were a sudden call – wasn't that what I said to 'ee, George?"

"That's what you said," Uden nodded.

"Folks, when I saw Zacchary bending down a-diggin' nigh the clump o' willows, up there in the churchyard, d'ye know the thought that came to me?"

The murmur following the question indicated that none of them claimed ability to follow Holley's mental processes.

"Why," the farmer continued, "my thought was on the first time I seen him on the old St. Lawrence ground at Canterbury, and how he druv the ball that day. He kept the Sussex chaps chasing about like a flock o' white new-clipped sheep running and stretching on their hind legs, and the ball a-sailing over their heads in among the elms like a frightened jay heading for her nest."

"'Tis cricket you're talking of: we don't take no notice of it," Zacchary Moss said in a tone of dismissal that roused Holley.

"There's a lot ye know nothing about on the Ma'sh," he rapped out. "But if some folks on the Ma'sh *had* learned to play cricket the Ma'sh would be a safer place to live in."

Here again was that hint of something lying. Behind, unseen.

"What I meant," Moss cried hotly, "was that I ain't seen any of this 'ere cricket, because I ain't no gadabout. A Ma'sh man I was born; a Ma'sh man I dies!" and he slapped the table with stiff defiance.

"Don't you heed 'im, sir," Vidler whispered to me. "Zacchary do go maggoty like that when crossed."

Holley, filling his pipe, went on reminiscently, as if there had been no interruption;

"Ah, well, that were more'n thirty years agone. But the bowler have got his wicket at last."

Uden, with portentous gravity, nodded agreement.

"Ay, so he have, Holley, so he have; the same Great Bowler as gets us all i' the end."

There was a moment's silence. Moss lifted his old hat from the table and, with cold dignity, placed it on his head. Then the man who had not yet spoken, knocking the ashes from his pipe, said quietly as he got to his feet:

"We knows who got 'im out. The question that's yet to settle is 'ow he was got out."

"Now, now, Mr. Apps," someone said warningly.

But I had heard enough. This, with all the other little straws that had moved since that morning, decided me.

A little later, when they had all gone, I took the road to New Romney and wired for McNab.

Chapter 6

McNab arrived at the Woolpack as I was sitting down to breakfast next morning. Well enough did I know the significance of the scrutiny he gave to my face while we shook hands. He wanted to know if I still remained as sure of the case as my wire had indicated. And on that score he seemed satisfied before I had uttered a word.

"All right," he said. "You can tell me about it after breakfast."

Refusing to utter another word, he planted himself down at the table.

As a matter of fact, I was more certain than I had been the night before that there was need for a very careful inquiry into the death of Mr. Cardew. It is true that immediately after despatching the telegram doubt assailed me. I had returned to Burrish and spent the evening in setting down on paper every item I had gleaned about the affair, and all the facts relevant to it, which had come within my knowledge. These I marshalled into a numbered sequence, and, looking at them, my last lingering doubt was dispelled. So, when I had reduced this dossier to the form of a questionnaire for McNab, I felt that this part of my task was complete.

There certainly was, as the lawyers say, a case to answer. After that, to pass the time, I had begun to construct an enlarged plan of the immediate neighbourhood from that section of a map of Kent I discovered in a ten-year-old County Directory, which was part of the sitting room furniture. Mrs. Beddoes found me at work on this, as I intended she should, when she entered to lay the supper. My occupation interested her, and, in consequence, I was able to get a considerable amount of information from her about the neighbourhood and the people.

Having taken care to have the drawing sufficiently advanced to show all the roads and dykes, so far as was possible from the small scale map, she indicated for me the exact position in which Redcotes, and a number of other houses, stood. By this means it was as natural as it was easy to gather much information about the people who lived in the houses I was setting down on my map.

The Woolpack itself seemed to stand in the centre of the Burrish world. It did so stand in the topographical sense at least. For, shorn of unessential details, the plan I drew showed a set of roads like the letter K, the Woolpack standing where the four roads meet. Thus, from the window at which I was sitting, I had the straight New Romney road on my left, the Dymchurch road on my right; but I had a better view of the other two roads, represented by the diagonal arms of the letter, the upper one being the road to Bonnington, high on the ridge which forms the northern side of the Marsh; the lower arm being the little frequented road that leads to Botolph Bridge.

This last road interested me most, when I learned from Mrs. Beddoes that on it, one mile away, stood the principal house in the parish, which was called Redcotes. And this information, after considerable talk on the late sad death of its owner, led to further talk on his family. Thus I learned that Windygate, where the married daughter resided, was on the Bonnington road, also about one mile from the Woolpack.

By this time Mrs. Beddoes' interest was really warm. She was flattered, I fancy, to be able to instruct the gentleman from London. I put down everything, even the position of the dozen or so cottages, mostly on the Dymchurch side, which made up the village, with the church and the churchyard, and Mr. Moss's cottage on my right, and the school (where the inquest was to be held) on my left, a little way up the New Romney road.

No, I was right; there were no other houses to put in on that road; but I must put in Mr. Rowland Todd's house on the Bonnington road, close to Windygate, but nearer Burrish. Other names, which meant nothing to me, she mentioned. But the name that was not mentioned was the one I most wanted to hear – the name of the motorcyclist, the supposed owner of the possibly important cigarette case. It must have been the only name Mrs. Beddoes omitted. The conclusion I came to was that Mr. Sneyd did not reside in Burrish. After that I had gone to bed content to have ready both a questionnaire on the significant facts and a plan of the terrain which would probably be useful to McNab.

And it was in that hope that, as soon as Mrs. Beddoes had ceased fussing over his needs and shut the door, that I produced the list and the drawing. McNab pushed his plate away and laid them on the table. His eyebrows lifted at sight of the map; but it was on the other document he began:

QUESTIONNAIRE, relative to the death of James Cardew, following on the suspicions of Miss Ann Cardew stated to us prior to that death.

A. The Police: do they entertain suspicion?

If not, how account for the inquest, their inquiries as to the cigarette case, their interest in the stick planted on the roadside; the measurements taken on the road where the cigarette case was found; their reticence?

Are the police suspicions derived from Miss Ann Cardew?

If so, why is she under police observation; why did Sergeant Strood refer to her in derogatory terms?

B. The Public. What significance attaches to:

Mr. Holley's saying about the insecurity of life on the Marsh; Mr. Apps' suggestion that his hearers knew who was responsible for Mr. Cardew's end, but not how it was brought about?

C. General Questions:

(1) Why did Sneyd deny ownership of the cigarette case after it had been identified as his by Miss Cardew?

(2) Why did Mr. Cardew leave that article on the road after stooping to examine it?

(3) Who, before George Jippling, last saw him alive?

(4) Where was Sneyd at that time?

How anxiously I watched McNab as he read may be imagined. Now and again I detected a glint in his dark eyes, and here and there they narrowed ominously. More than once he paused over a question; but in vain I strove to see at which. Towards the end he smiled, laid down my questionnaire, and, while feeling for his tobacco pouch, looked over at me in kindly fashion.

"Doing a bit of detection on your own account, for once in a way?"

"What do you mean?"

"Only that you seem to have made up your mind not only that murder has been done, but also as to who the murderer is."

"Was that going too far, McNab?"

"But why do you suggest this Sneyd is the man? This Mr. Apps, I infer, mentioned no name when he said they knew who was responsible."

Then I had to explain the circumstances under which Apps had spoken of Mr. Cardew, as one whose innings had been ended by the great bowler, Death. The point in the entry, I said, was that there seemed to be a belief, common to all his hearers, that Mr. Cardew had been got rid of illegitimately. McNab's face cleared as I retold that talk.

"But why do you fasten on to Sneyd?" he asked. "Is it because you saw him under police observation?"

"No, because of the cigarette case."

"Same thing. Undoubtedly their action is due to his denial of ownership. And they are quite right. But, even if you can prove it is his property, that does not carry us far, since Sneyd may be denying ownership for reasons quite unconnected with Cardew's death."

I felt shattered. But he hadn't yet finished with me.

"As to why Cardew left the cigarette case lying on the road, surely the natural explanation is that, if the act of stooping induced the heart attack from which it is said he died a few minutes later, he would hardly bother much about a cigarette case."

"Anything more?" I asked in despair. "Go on; don't mind me."

But he did not appear to have even heard me as he began to pace the floor.

"As for the mysterious stick, any child may have stuck it in and left it there."

"Precisely what Strood said," I admitted.

McNab looked up sharply, and stopped dead.

"He did, did he? That's worth knowing. And yet he got an inquest despite the medical certificate of death from heart failure? Now that is one of the facts with real significance."

"Can you infer anything useful from it?" I asked.

For the first time he perceived my, I suppose, crestfallen aspect. All the same he laughed.

"Useful?" he queried, head on one side. "Well, there's one thing I infer, and that is that Sergeant Strood got out of your clutch without telling half as much as he could have done. No fool, that sergeant! We'll have a talk with him after the inquest."

"But," I said, greatly astonished. "if you are staying for the inquest—"

"Well?"

"I mean, you seem to have found answers to all my vital questions. You have torn my questionnaire to shreds."

He shook his head.

"No, I have given possible answers. But are they the true answers? Your questions still stand; there's not one on the list that does not cry aloud for an answer. Apart, any single one might not count for much, but, taken together and in combination, they seem decisive."

He had crossed over and taken up the plan I had drawn of the neighbourhood.

"Then?"

"Then—" he repeated abstractedly.

"You think it's" – I could no more than whisper the word—"murder?"

A curt nod was the only response.

"Who lives at the house you've marked Broadmead?"

"One Rowland Todd."

"What is he?"

"Don't know. Mrs. Beddoes simply mentioned him."

"And at Windygate?"

"Mr. Percy Campbell."

"Ah, yes, the son-in-law. I remember."

I, too, remembered – remembered, that is, the queer look that had come over McNab's face when this man's name had first been mentioned – a look that had been repeated when his brother Cyril's name came up.

"McNab, you suspect him," I said.

"I do! But not of murder. Though," he added grimly, "one might suspect a Percy or a Cyril Campbell of anything. Heaven help us! What names to tack on to the name of a Campbell – Percy and Cyril. Ian and Archibald if you like; but – oh Innisbuie – Percy and Cyril! Shades of Ben Cruachan!"

Then I knew what he meant. His dislike of an Anglicised fellow-countryman was almost ferocious in its intensity. This peculiar trait in him I first discovered through his distaste for Matheson, my chief on the *Record*. As I have stated elsewhere, the one thing I entirely liked about Matheson was that it pleased him to be mistaken for an Englishman. It therefore took me some time to discover that McNab's distaste for Matheson was, unlike my own, not personal but representative: Matheson as a type, not as an individual. What McNab suspected in the Campbells, Percy and Cyril, was, I now knew, merely the crime of their type, the crime of trying to be more English than the

English. To my thinking it was a harmless, even a praiseworthy ambition; but to McNab a trait so black in itself as to make the brothers seem in his eyes capable of anything. It was for this reason I there and then made a mental note to discount, or head off, McNab from any unfounded suspicions he might form concerning either of the Campbells. For well I knew the disabling effect a strong prejudice can exert on a mind highly efficient and unbiased in all other respects.

An hour passed in question and discussion. At the end he had become familiar with every detail I had gleaned since my arrival. As the hour fixed for the inquest approached he got more and more restless. The symptom was familiar to me. McNab was no cold-blooded calculating machine, but a very human organism, apt to suffer from acute nervous tension before, so to speak, going "over the top." Several times he pulled out and re-examined the map of the district I had drawn. Continually in the last quarter of an hour his eye went to the slow-moving hands of the clock.

"This is going to be a queer case," he said, so obviously to himself that I just sat and watched.

"The whole of Burrish will be in the schoolroom," I reminded him.

He nodded.

"I'm counting on that. I must not be seen."

Before I could speak, he added, "Yes, perhaps you'd better go now."

"Aren't you coming?"

"No; later, perhaps. Not yet. There's something I've got just one chance to ascertain while all Burrish is at the inquest. And there won't be another such chance – unless we have another inquest."

So I left him alone in the Woolpack.

Chapter 7

THOUGH the schoolroom by the time I reached it was crowded to suffocation, Sergeant Strood saw to it that a seat was found for me. The coroner was late, Strood whispered, probably through a miscalculation of the distance, he not being their usual official. As I looked round the room an elbow nudged me in the ribs. Turning, at my left side I perceived the little man, Uden, whose greeting, though reduced by the gravity of the occasion to a solemn nod, was meant to be friendly. I was glad to have him there: he might be useful. Presently I had picked out, in different parts of the room, Mr. Holley, Apps and Vidler, and, near the door beside the constable, Zacchary Moss himself. Mrs. Beddoes and young Ben I also saw, but in vain I sought for the faces of the two others I could have identified – Miss Ann Cardew and Sneyd.

Another violent nudge from Uden.

"T'other side, there, against th' wall, that be Mr. Campbell."

It would have been hard to miss seeing him, for all eyes were turned on him as he headed the group of people who were being piloted by P.C. Hackett towards the bench reserved for those who had to give evidence. First in a line of five people who followed Hackett, he walked with downcast head, carrying his bowler hat against his breast. Behind him came a lady of mature years, dressed in black, whom I judged to be Miss Cardew. She was followed by two young, well-dressed men. The last figure in the little procession was a stoutish old man, of the labouring class, in his Sunday clothes, whom I took to be Jippling.

The group came to rest on a bench almost opposite to me, so I had them in full view. I wondered which of the other two men was Cyril Campbell. On such an occasion not much could be made out from their faces, for all, even Jippling, maintained that grave, statuesque rigidity of expression which transforms the living face into a cold, stone image. The group, in fact, was only saved from complete immobility by Miss Cardew's hand, which from time to time lifted a handkerchief, its whiteness startlingly exaggerated against all that black, to dab away a tear.

Presently, however, the gaze of one or other of the men lifted from the floor, and for a moment his eyes would sidle discreetly round the room. Hackett mounted on a chair and opened the window behind them with a noise that was like a scream. After that the general whispering around me began again. An odour of camphor reached me from Jippling's Sunday clothes.

"Which is Mr. Cyril Campbell?" I murmured in Uden's ear.

"Next seat to Miss Cardew," he whispered sibilantly back.

"Who's the other?"

"Next to Jarge Jippling?"

"Yes."

I was trying to identify this man with Sneyd. He was not unlike, if the difference in the clothes, and the change in facial expression, were taken into account.

"That 'un be Mr. Rowland Todd."

All three were young, though Percy Campbell was just noticeably older than Cyril. The two younger men, who sat together, were more like brothers, with much the same rather sharp features and black hair. At least as I then saw them.

But Percy Campbell, with his more open countenance, fresh complexion and reddish, auburn hair, was quite unlike either, except in build, in which he did resemble Cyril, Todd being considerably slighter in chest and shoulder.

My study of them was broken off when the delayed deputy-coroner came bustling in, carrying a bundle of documents in one hand and his pince-nez in the other. By the time all the, to me, familiar preliminaries were got through it was a quarter to twelve. I wondered just what McNab was then up to. My thought was that it must be something of first-rate importance since to achieve it he was ready to risk missing much at the inquest.

At first, however, and for a considerable time, there did not seem very much to miss. Mr. Percy Campbell, the first witness, gave the formal evidence of identification. He had last seen the deceased alive about 11 a.m. on the day of his death. That was at Windygate. Yes, Mr. Cardew then seemed in his normal health. No, his visit was very short. He had come for an address which he, witness, did not know, though his brother Cyril did. His brother, however, was away in Folkestone, and though expected back at any moment, Mr. Cardew did not wait. Witness undertook to get the address from his brother and telephone it to Redcotes before they left for London later in the day.

"I understand you forgot to do so," the coroner said.

"That is so. My brother was so late we had barely time to catch the 2.5 at Appledore, and in the hurry the whole thing escaped my memory till about seven o'clock, in the hotel in London. The hotel was the Norfolk, in Howard Street. I then went to my brother's room and got the required address from his address book, which was Hotel Riposo, Brighton."

"You did not telephone it from the hotel?"

"No, I did not telephone at all, I went out and wired it from the Southampton Street office."

"So I understand. Would it not have been quicker, and more convenient to yourself, to have telephoned from the hotel?"

While the witness hesitated, the coroner put his pince-nez to his nose and surveyed him, playfully smiling.

"Was it, perhaps, that a trunk telephone call would have cost more, Mr. Campbell?"

A titter, which in other circumstances would have been a guffaw, ran round the court. Campbell flushed perceptibly.

"No," he said, "it wasn't that. It was because I could not be sure that at that hour Mr. Cardew himself would receive my call, and I was afraid a domestic might not take it down correctly."

The coroner nodded, pleased with the effect of his witticism.

"I see. Hotel Riposo, Brighton. Yes, I see. As the essential word in the address is a French word, you considered it safer to have it written down by the post office rather than the parlour-maid. That was very thoughtful of you, very thoughtful."

Campbell bowed.

"That was why. You see, sir," he went on confidentially, "I know it isn't everyone who can recognise an Italian word when they hear it."

If the sarcasm was lost on most of the audience, the coroner did not miss it. It was his turn to flush.

"Ah, well," he weakly said, "the question of relative speed as between the telephone and telegraph did not matter much after all." He lifted an authoritative hand. "You may stand down, Mr. Campbell."

What I liked in Percy Campbell was the quiet, deft thrust by which he had got his own back on the coroner.

Miss Cardew, so far as I then saw, added little to what was already known. Her brother had not been well for some time. Yes, she thought he himself was concerned about his health. She thought so because he appeared nervous lest his feet should get wet. He had got into the habit of examining his shoes to see if they were damp. No, that was not the only symptom she had observed. Another was that he had now come to dread the night air, and against his former custom had latterly shut his window on retiring.

Yes, she recalled last Wednesday. He was not more unsettled than usual. She knew about the address. He had told her, and she had seen the letter ready sealed lying on the table, with only the name of the person on it. The name was that of Mr. Rowland Todd. Her brother did fret over not getting the address sooner. But very little had seemed to agitate him lately. It was almost nine when the telegram arrived. He then, when he had added the words, Hotel Riposo, Brighton, to the envelope, went out to post the letter. That was the last time she saw him alive.

Cyril Campbell, next called, confirmed his brother's evidence. But he had not seen Mr. Cardew on the day of his death. He knew about Mr. Cardew's indifferent health. But he himself had so recently returned from India that he could not judge how much this had altered him. On hearing of certain symptoms from a member of the family he had suspected cardiac disease, and had advised consultation with Dr. Jones. The deceased was said to be "touchy "about interference, and his own position was a delicate one.

Mr. Rowland Todd said he had known the deceased for the last nine months. Mr. Cardew was an old friend of his father's, and he had shown him much kindness since he, witness, had come to Burrish. He had last seen Mr. Cardew alive about ten days ago, before leaving for Reading, from which place, he, witness, had written to him, in reply to a letter received from Mr. Cardew at that place, the letter which, he believed, was now in the coroner's possession. Mr. Cyril Campbell knew witness's address because there had been some talk of their spending that weekend together at Brighton. As it happened this had not been possible; and Mr. Cardew's second letter addressed to him at the "Riposo" had been redirected to Burrish. No, he could not produce it. It was merely a letter expressing a desire that he should return at once to Burrish, and, as he had already returned before receiving the letter, he had judged it to be of no importance and had destroyed it. As a matter of fact, he had got home on the morning following the death, and had only learned of the sad event on his way to Redcotes.

When, after that, Mr. Todd stood down, I racked my brains to find a reason as to why he had been called. Then, just as the name of George Jippling was cried, the explanation began to dawn. The significance of Mr. Todd's appearance before the court must lie in the letter sent by him to Mr. Cardew from Reading. But why, then, had that letter not been read? Obviously because something lay behind which, at this stage, the police did not wish to have disclosed. That could be the only explanation. He had contributed absolutely nothing relevant to the inquiry, otherwise. Few of those present might be aware of that, but I was too well versed in inquests not to be startled over Mr. Rowland Todd's evidence.

Jippling, a little, thickset barrel of a man, with grey side-whiskers, seemed to sweat nervousness as he stood up. The prominent Adam's apple in his throat moved up and down as he tried to moisten his dry throat, and all the moisture appeared to have converged to his shiny, red, honest countenance.

"Now, Mr. Jippling," the coroner said, "just tell us all you know or what you saw last Wednesday when Mr. Cardew came along the road."

"Last Wensday," Jippling began, "my clock, it give me a bit of a fright like, it being—"

"Your what?" the coroner cried, looking up.

"My clock, zur. What with 'ur beginning to get a bit of old age on 'er, like 'er master, ye see, she 'ad taken to—"

"This is not an inquest on your clock, Mr. Jippling; be as concise as you can," the coroner interrupted severely.

Jippling may have guessed the meaning of concise, but he seemed incapable of telling his story in any other fashion than that in which he had rehearsed it to all the neighbourhood previously.

"It were like this, zur," he resumed. "That there clock of mine, she being old, ain't to be depended on. So every night now I goes to my door for to hear the church clock a'strike – about ten, that is. Las' Wensday I goes out as usual, and as I was standing there a-listening I see a man coming down the road from Burrish way. After a bit I saw 'twas Mr. Cardew; and the next thing was I see him stop short, and then bend down a'most double to look at his feet. Then, just as I was wondering what it might be, I hear him give a sudden cry, and straighten himself. Next I sees him stagger about like a man what had lost his balance. Then he come on again. I left the porch where I were standing, and goes down to my garden gate so's—"

"One moment. Did you see anyone else on the road?"

"There weren', nobody."

"Now, Mr. Jippling, be very careful about your answer to this question: Could you have seen anyone? Was it not quite dark?"

"Not dark wi' the moon at full, zur; and I knowing what could and could not be seen in a mile around my cottage."

"Did Mr. Cardew seem to think there was anyone there?"

"He did, zur; leeastaways, I did see 'im look behind him, mor'n once, as he come towards me. That's what made me look very careful."

"And you are positive no one was there?"

Jippling was emphatic about that.

"Sartin sure. There weren't no mortal there, and there couldn't be, not without me a-seein' of him."

"Very well, go on with your story."

"Well, zur, Mr. Cardew, as soon as 'ee sees me at th' gate, 'ee stops dead. It were on the tip of my tongue to ask if anything had scared him. But I didn't, for I saw that a question like that would 'ave been rude, from me to him. Then, before I could think of anything else to say, Mr. Cardew 'ee come over all of a sudden, and says to me, very low, 'Jippling, tell me, do you see anyone on the road?' ee says, breathing mighty quick. 'No, zur,' I says, 'there bain't nobody on the road.' And no more there weren't. I could see a'most to the Woolpack, and even a water-rat couldn't a-crossed th' road without me a'seein' of him. Mr. Cardew gave a little laugh then, 'Thought myself there couldn't really be,' he says.

Then he says, 'Goodnight' to me with a wave of the hand, and goes on in at the Redcotes gate. I stood still, watching him close.

"What made you watch him?" the coroner asked abruptly.

"Well, zur, I 'ad come out to hear the clock strike ten, and it' adn't yet. But it weren't that that kept me there neither. It were the queerness of it all, the feeling that something had happened that I – well, zur" – George Jippling shook his head in bewilderment— "something just mighty queer about it all."

"Can you explain to us the foundation of that feeling?"

Jippling sighed plaintively.

"'Tain't no bit of use, zur. I've tried often since."

The coroner frowned.

"You were just scared yourself, it seems to me, and most unreasonably, since you can assign no cause."

This Jippling admitted.

"That's true, zur, scared I was, and without being able to put a name to it."

"Well, proceed with what follows," the coroner said, "and please confine yourself to stating only what you saw or heard."

It was clear he did not himself attach importance to the vague fears of an illiterate yokel on a moonlight night. And Jippling, who felt the contempt without, as he might himself have said, being able to put a name to it, proceeded.

"The next thing I saw was Mr. Cardew going right across the lawn what he'd just had top-dressed with sand. Seeing that, it was my fancy he—"

"Facts, please, not fancies," the coroner interjected, "we've had too many fancies already."

"The next thing I saw was Mr. Cardew stumble and fall," Jippling continued breathlessly. "When he didn't get up I started to cross the road to go in at the gate. I could see him lying, and he didn't move. I kept my eyes on him all the time. I didn't go very fast, for I was expecting him to get on his feet every minute. But he didn't, he lay quiet and never made a sound."

"You heard no sound of any description?"

"Nothing, excep' what I'd come out to hear, the church clock striking ten. That was just as I was a-crossing the lawn, and in that quietness, zur, it sounded just like th' passing bell; it made me feel 'ee was gone before I got to him. And 'ee were to," Jipping burst out as the coroner's forefinger lifted in reproof. "What I felt then were right, anyway," he declared almost defiantly.

This ended George Jippling's evidence. My conclusion, from the coroner's manner, was that he held Jippling responsible for all the vague gossip, floating around, which had entailed his own presence there in the absence of the regular official for the district.

The next witness, Dr. Jones, of Appledore, said he had treated the deceased for cardiac weakness for some time previous to his death. In his younger days Mr. Cardew had been an athlete, and occasionally that told adversely on a man in later life. He had, however, not anticipated any immediate danger. No, he was not altogether surprised on being called to Redcotes on Wednesday to find Mr. Cardew dead. He had heard the evidence of the previous witness. As to the cry on the road heard by that witness, it was just such a cry as might come from one at the moment of a sudden heart attack, induced by the act of stooping. One could never tell in such cases. A little undue physical exertion, mental strain, or worry even, reacted so prejudicially; and not infrequently with fatal results. He was quite satisfied that death was due to syncope.

Police Constable Hackett's evidence was still more formal. He testified briefly to having been called on the night in question to Redcotes. He had examined the body and found on it no marks of external injury of any kind.

This concluded the evidence. But, just when I was expecting the coroner to announce a verdict of death from natural causes, there came a surprise. Sergeant Strood and another officer in an inspector's uniform, whom I had not before observed, approached the table.

The three put their heads together, and conversed for rather a long time in low tones. My own experience led me to suspect what was coming. But the others around me appeared to think something had gone wrong with the procedure, and the whispering increased while they waited. Of the witnesses only Miss Cardew had left after giving her evidence, and those who remained, the two Campbells, Todd and Jippling, watched the official conference intently, as persons who, having played their separate parts in the proceedings, had a special concern in seeing that nothing now went wrong.

At last the officers stood back. The coroner lifted his head and cleared his throat.

"This court," he said, "is adjourned for seven days, to enable the police time for further necessary investigations."

Chapter 8

We sat up late that night in the inn parlour. It was Saturday night, and that, taken with the inquest earlier in the day, brought a large company to gossip over the Woolpack ale. Not till they had gone, and the lights were out, and the door locked, could we do anything. But where we sat it was quite safe to talk. We had the long, low, odd-shaped parlour to ourselves. And certainly I had plenty to talk about that day.

McNab had not, after all, put in an appearance at the inquest. From this I had inferred he was out on some very engrossing investigations. My surprise was therefore very great when, on entering the Woolpack about two, after the inquest proceedings were over, I found him already there. Not only that: he was seated at the table, having a bread and cheese lunch with Mary Beddoes. They were laughing together. I did not know what to think. Of Mary I had caught several glimpses since my arrival, but never more than a glimpse, for invariably at sight of me she disappeared round the corner of a passage, or melted behind a door.

Shy as a squirrel with strangers, she was a slim, very long-legged girl for her age, which was, her mother had told me, ten, though later she herself claimed to be ten and a half. Mary alone of the Woolpack household had no desire to attend the inquest – probably because it was held in the over-familiar schoolroom.

Mrs. Beddoes and Ben, entering with me, seemed no less surprised. But their surprise had a different cause: it astonished them to find McNab reveal so little interest in the inquest. Certainly, if McNab wanted to prove himself a stranger devoid of all concern in Burrish affairs, he could not have taken a better course; nor with a person better suited to publish the fact than the landlady. But I was too annoyed to see that at the moment.

"What have you been up to?" I demanded when the child had fled.

"Down to would be the better term," he replied, pushing back his chair.

Then I caught sight of the book that lay on the armchair by the window, and I became yet more annoyed, for it was a copy of *Alice in Wonderland*. And it was his own copy too, as I saw when I picked it up. He had actually carried the book with him from London! I held it out to him accusingly.

"Yes, indeed, 'down to' would be the better term. McNab, have you really been wasting time reading this to that child?"

"No, just showing her the pictures; the letterpress is beyond her yet."

"But not behind you, it seems."

"I hope not," he said with ludicrous fervour. He began to roll a cigarette.

This was one of his foibles that I could endure, though I found it hard to comprehend why he should roll his own cigarettes. With his deft fingers he made them quite well, but not nearly so well as one could buy them ready made. He had told me he did it because he liked the finest quality of paper, but I suspected it was because he got about one and a half more cigarettes for his money. Then he looked up.

"I'm sure Mrs. Beddoes isn't scowling like that," he said, smiling.

"Probably not. She wouldn't, of course, think your time wasted on her brat," I rejoined.

"Yet she's thinking exactly what you think. She left me in this room when she hurried away to the inquest, and she found me here when she returned. So she makes exactly the same childish assumption that you have made, which is that I have been here all the time."

That wasn't quite true. What I was annoyed at was to think that he could evidently have come in for part of the inquest at least; but it had sufficient truth in it to make me wince. He pushed me into the armchair.

"What could the inquest tell me that I don't already suspect, or that, at least, you and Sergeant Strood, when he comes here tonight, can tell me?"

"Strood coming here tonight – but you haven't spoken to him yet!" I said, surprised. McNab waved an impatient hand.

"Haven't even seen him, but I expect him to obey the instructions the Chief will have already telephoned. Don't bother about that! Strood will come here tonight just as soon as he can come without being seen. What you have to get into your silly head is this." Standing over me, his voice suddenly lost its impatient note and became very grave. "If this is murder, it is no common murder. That, at least, you would learn at the inquest. If there is a criminal in it at all, he is no ordinary man. That tells us something at the start. Among other things it tells us we must go warily, full of eyes. Compared with an ordinary case, Mr. Godfrey Chance, this is like the difference between fishing and shooting. In shooting you, more or less, know the game you're after; you put him up and on the wing, then bring him down; but in fishing you never see your fish, though you may know he is there."

He paused, and as I looked up at his face the flicker of a smile quavered about his lips.

"When I was a boy I used to be quite a good angler. Good training for a detective. We used to have pike-catching competitions, and many a vicious trout-devouring brute I've landed from the Teith just above the old bridge at Callander. Often I won the prize for the heaviest fish, for, among other things, I took care to keep out of sight, and to fish from the north bank so as to cast no shadow upon the water.

"Now, Chance" – his mouth was again stern – "that comedy of yours with Strood among the rushes was a mistake. You were seen in talk with him; the fact was commented on, as you afterwards found, in connection with this very case. We must have no more shadows on the waters. That is why I could not afford to show any interest in the inquest today. First impressions count for so much in country places. They're mightily curious about a stranger to begin with; but, once sized up, it is seldom they can be got to readjust their earliest judgment of him. And that," he concluded, "is a fact which may give me more liberty of movement later on. Now, when I saw Miss Ann Cardew just an hour ago—"

But Mrs. Beddoes entered at this point with my own lunch. While she was busy coming and going I gave McNab an account of the inquest, and in this the landlady certainly showed far greater interest than McNab.

"So you've seen Miss Ann?" I said as soon as we were alone.

"Had to. She knows me. I argued she would not be at the inquest. They would get the brother-in-law to identify; and she was away, like the Campbells themselves, when the thing happened. After seeing her, I went to Dymchurch to ring up the Chief, and then returned to wind up by having a look at the scene of the tragedy."

"You got all that in while the inquest was on?"

"I took young Ben's cycle. And your sketch plan saved much time; that and the fact that the population was gathered into the schoolroom saved me from wasting time in taking precautions."

Then a thought came to me.

"Do you realise that the sergeant suspects Sneyd?" I asked.

"What of that?"

"Only this: my comedy with Strood, as you called it, did at least show me that Miss Ann and Sneyd met by appointment."

"Well, if that proves anything, it is that she, as against Strood, doesn't suspect Robert Sneyd. As a matter of fact, she does not suspect Sneyd; but she became aware of Strood's suspicions through the inquiries he was making about the cigarette case, and she was meeting Sneyd to tell him about it when you saw them together."

I began to see daylight.

"And it was to warn her not to know you when you met that you went to Redcotes?"

He hesitated.

"That, of course; but I also went to get a free hand."

"A free hand?"

"Free from all concern with her interests. That was essential if I was to work with the authorities. I found her with no interest one way or the other. Poor girl, she simply wanted to avert a tragedy. Now that failed she does not care what happens."

I think he forgot my presence at this point. Covertly, I watched him as he began, hands deep in pockets, to pace the floor. What was whirling in his mind? Just so I had seen him in an earlier case.

"McNab, you got hold of something."

He came back, startled.

"What did you say?" he asked.

"You've got hold of something – you've found out something this morning. What is it?" A phrase he had used earlier came back to me – a phrase I had mocked earlier. But now I saw its significance. "You went down to something in the dyke," I said. "You've found something – something tangible."

"Tangible?" he repeated. "It's something you can touch, anyway; but can you connect it with the case?"

As I rose hurriedly he drew something from his pocket. It was a broad piece of blue velvet ribbon, about four inches long; sewn to the centre was a small rubber band.

"Make anything of it?"

I didn't try.

"That all you got?"

In dumb reply he produced a collection of scraps of paper, chiefly pieces torn from newspapers, such oddments as get blown by the winds and would be finally trapped in any water-logged ditch.

"Nothing to write home about in that lot," I said in disgust.

"Very likely," he replied. "And so, if you've finished eating, we'll go and inspect the interior of the church, or something like that."

Not another word would he say. But we did not view the church. Instead we went for a long walk – a long walk with a very silent McNab. And this, if it did nothing to satisfy my curiosity, served, in time, to steady my nerves. At least it did so till the hour approached when Sergeant Strood became due at the Woolpack.

They grew noiser round in the bar as the night wore on. The sound of their voices came along the wall from the tap-room, which was a modern adjunct at the end of the house proper. McNab was absorbed in some writing. Towards ten the sound of the bar door being shut came with an increasing frequency as, one by one, the visitors kept leaving. The church clock striking ten was the signal for a general exodus on to the road. There were prolonged leave-takings, the scrunching of feet on the gritty road as the separate groups took their various ways, and lastly, in the stillness, came the sound of Ben on his rounds, locking up for the night.

When he had mounted the stairs I slipped over to the window and, with the curtain at my back, stood watching the road. Half an hour I must have watched like that. Then at last I saw something coming rapidly down the road. It was Sergeant Strood, on his bicycle. He swept across towards the door as silently as a hawk at night, his great bulk no more than a flying shadow on the moonlit road.

Chapter 9

Sergeant Strood, in response to McNab's gesture, slipped into the chair opposite. I took the head of the table, having the two, who faced each other, on either side of me. The sergeant put his peaked cap softly on the floor at his feet.

"We can talk freely?" he asked with lifted eyebrows.

"Quite; their bedrooms are at the far end of the upper passage, overlooking the churchyard."

McNab motioned me to act as host, and as I poured out the whisky from the bottle at my right hand I wondered how McNab, who had only arrived that morning, could have known just where the Beddoes slept. Some of the official stiffness left Strood as I filled the glasses. Probably he had been wondering as to the footing on which he was to confer with this man from London, about whom the Chief had telephoned such precise instructions.

"Meet anyone?" McNab asked.

"Only two, sir – Tom Vidler and William Apps by name; beyond Newlyns, that was. But I heard them long before they could see me, and hid till they passed." He turned to me, holding up his glass. "That pair had too much of this to see me."

"So you didn't have to tell them part of what you knew," I said.

Strood twinkled a knowing eye at me as the glass went to his lips.

"We have to follow instructions – to the best of our ability."

"Quite right," McNab agreed. "You received instructions for tonight?"

"I did, sir. My instructions are to let you know all we know, and to accept such help as you care to give."

"Good. Then we'll hammer the whole case out here and now." McNab lifted one of the candles and applied it to his pipe. The mere sight of that pipe warned me we were in for serious business. A cigarette with him was no more than a substitute for a smoke – a whiff in a moment of relaxation. The five candles on the big, broad table which formed our sole illumination were there at his suggestion. And Mrs. Beddoes had retired with an easier mind in consequence; for she had not at all liked the notion of leaving her two inexperienced London gentlemen in sole charge of an unfamiliar paraffin lamp.

"Go ahead, sergeant," McNab nodded as he set down the candlestick; "give us the situation as it now stands."

Strood placed his elbows on the table and then breathed out a sigh of perplexity.

"It's queer at the moment, this affair is. Dr. Jones was ready to certify death from heart failure when Dr. Campbell stepped in. There had been a lot of talk, mostly due to the fright Jippling got; his telling about Mr. Cardew glancing back and asking if he'd seen anyone; and to the inquiries Hackett got busy making. Started the folks' tongues, they did, between them. That, I reckon, was what brought Dr. Campbell in. And Dr. Jones thinks a lot of him on account of his high medical qualifications. So when Dr. Campbell, to stop the talk as it were, insisted on a post-mortem, Dr. Jones gave way, and we've just had it."

"And found?"

"Nothing – nothing, that is, except what they expected."

"Yet you aren't going to drop the case?"

"No, not till we know more. After all, sir, to say a man has died from heart failure, that, to my mind, is like saying he has died from want of breath, which is what we all die of, sooner or later, even though we aren't strangled. But I dare say my superintendent would have accepted Dr. Jones's certificate all right except for that one other thing that is bothering us."

"The cigarette case?"

"That's right – the cigarette case it is. We've done a mighty lot of thinking about that; for there's more in it than you might surmise, believe me. It seems a mighty small thing to hang a case on, though."

"Not too small," McNab cut in. "I've seen a man hanged for a blade of grass."

"A blade of grass!" Strood stared. There were so many blades of grass on the Marsh.

"Yes, a blade of green grass where no blade of such a fresh, green grass should have been at the time."

"Ah, that's it! That's talking!" Strood thumped his clenched fist enthusiastically on the table. "The freshness of the blade timed the chap, I suppose – proved where he had been when he said he hadn't been. I'd like to hear about that."

"Another time, sergeant. Go on with the cigarette case. Very little that's green about it, I fancy," McNab concluded, almost *sotto voce*.

The last muttered words appeared to astonish the sergeant. He sat considering them for a moment, his elbows on the table, his heavily moulded, high-coloured face thrown into strong relief against the dark, vague background. Strood had unbuttoned the upper half of his tunic, and the soft candlelight turned the buttons into spots of silver on his great chest.

"Now, sir, that's exactly what we did think about that business with the cigarette case – about that being green, I mean. Green as lush grass we set that young man down as being."

"Robert Sneyd?"

Strood nodded a slow, thoughtful assent as he produced a cardboard box from which he pushed the sheath and revealed a silver cigarette case inside. The box he slid across to McNab.

McNab inspected the case without touching it. Strood continued:

"Well, sir, you know the facts about the finding of that case by Hackett, and how it was identified by Miss Ann Cardew. What you may not know is that Hackett took the case round to Sneyd at the cottage where he has rooms at Littlestone, alongside the golf links. Hackett, saying nothing about where it had been got, said only it had been found, and that he had been told it was his – Mr. Sneyd's – property. The young fellow at once said this was wrong; or he hadn't lost his case. Now Hackett hadn't yet shown him the case. But what he had done was to apply the graphite to it, and already he'd got a photograph taken of the fingerprints the graphite threw up."

"How many?" McNab asked.

"Two only; thumb and finger of one hand. Here they are."

Strood, removing a pocket book from the inside of his half-opened tunic, extracted a couple of photographic prints. I passed them to McNab, who fished out his pocket lens.

"Hackett fancies he got quite a lot out o' that," the sergeant remarked while McNab remained bent over the table with the lens at his eye, like a watchmaker peering into the interior of a watch. Each photograph showed a different side of the cigarette case, and on each there was a black smudge, veined with innumerable convergent lines and circles, the one a thumb and the other a fingermark. McNab at last laid down his lens. Strood regarded him expectantly.

"This cigarette case was never lost," he said.

"Hackett says so too," the sergeant nodded.

"It was placed on the ground deliberately."

"That's what Hackett says."

"The owner is left-handed."

"By George, Hackett got that too!" Strood breathed in wonder.

"He is, I should guess, a man at least fairly well-to-do."

"Ah, Hackett didn't get that, though. I'll tell him."

"Don't blame him; it's only a guess," McNab smiled. "He's a man to encourage, this young constable."

"Hackett's what you might call an enthusiast. He don't need any encouraging. Just a little inclined to pride, Hackett is. And don't he love to see further than his superiors – and let them know it too, in the quiet, polite, little way he has."

But I wasn't keen to hear about Hackett.

"For Heaven's sake explain," I said. "If you can show the case never was lost, that has an important bearing on the whole affair."

McNab pushed the two photographs under my nose.

"Look at the two imprints," he said, "and tell me for what purpose the case was extracted from his pocket."

"To get a cigarette, surely."

"But it was empty."

"He had forgotten, probably."

"Then he wouldn't remember that until he opened it."

"Quite so."

"But he never opened it. If he had he would have left other imprints besides these two. Before he took it from his pocket the case had rubbed itself clean of fingerprints previously made against the wash-leather lining of his left waistcoat pocket. Now look at—"

"Half a moment, if you please, sir," Strood interrupted deprecatingly. "Young Hackett didn't know what the lining was, and if you'd explain to me, sir, how you got that, I'd be pleased to explain it to young Hackett."

McNab thought for a moment, the twitch about his mouth showing me that he too appreciated the sergeant's eagerness to be in a position to explain things to his subordinate. Then he pushed over the cardboard box and the two prints, which I placed between the sergeant and myself.

"Observe that case, sergeant, so bright and shiny. But not with the brightness of new silver. You've no doubt noticed that new silver has a bright quality, a soft sheen peculiar to itself, which wears off after use. This isn't a recent purchase, yet it is quite free of scratches and dents. So it has been kept in a pocket in which it did not come into contact with other articles. That at once suggests a vest pocket. More than that: it was kept in a pocket which fitted its size well enough to allow it to lie longitudinally, the hinged end in the bottom of the pocket, and yet loosely enough to permit of some friction against the pocket's lining. Observe next what the photographs show. Notice how neatly the fingers took the case from the pocket, the thumb going in next to the body, the forefinger outside, and both exactly over the snap-catch, that is right at the top edge. It is quite clear the case stood flat against the body. Had it been taken from any other than a vest pocket I should not have expected to see the grip so neat, or so well placed. In a bigger pocket there would have been evidences of fumbling, probably, and the fingerprints would have been lower down. Had that happened, and other imprints been made on the case, it would not have been evidence that the case was deliberately removed from the pocket in order to be placed in the position on the road where Mr. Cardew found it."

Strood, his face flushed, nodded vigorously.

"That's good; that *is* good! The chap didn't take it out to open it."

"No. You can take out such a case with finger and thumb, but you use the fingers of both hands to open it. All that is simple. The next question is: which of the two vest pockets was it kept in? It is certain it was *not* kept in a small upper pocket, for, as the fingerprints show, the case rested longitudinally, and the upper pocket is too small to carry a case of this size in that position. Was it in the right or left vest pocket? My conviction is that it was in the left; that is, in the pocket in which a watch is usually carried."

"That is not based on intuition?" I inquired.

"It is based on an observation of the brightness of the case, and on the fact that all trace of any previous handling had been polished off by friction in the pocket. But which pocket? Good tailors nowadays usually line the pocket on the left with selvyt, or wash-leather. And in such a pocket, especially if subject to" – he hesitated as if for a word, his eyes on Strood – "especially if subject to considerable vibration – on a motorcycle, say – the fingerprints put on the case before its final removal from the pocket would be obliterated. Now, which hand did he use to remove the case? One that did not stretch across his body, I say. Look at these photographs again and you see the thumb and finger descended vertically, from above, on to the upper edge of the case as it lay in the pocket. Had the fingers come across the body they would have gripped it in a more or less diagonal direction. Try it for yourself. You can do it without the slanting grip, but only if you bend or elevate your wrist to an angle not natural. Therefore, I infer that he used the hand nearest the pocket, and that was the left hand."

"Then," I said, "where did he keep his watch?"

"If not on his wrist, in his right-hand pocket; that is, in the pocket opposite to that in which the watch is invariably carried by right-handed people. As for my guess at his condition – this is a cigarette case of good, solid, unshowy quality; and cheap tailors do not specially line the watch pocket. Besides, those imprints seem to indicate, as far as they can, a person of refinement; but as to his condition there is nothing decisive."

McNab, having finished, reached for the decanter. To my mind the only point of first-rate importance was that which McNab appeared to have completely established: the fact that the cigarette case had been deliberately put on the road to attract Mr. Cardew's attention. But this was indeed a fact of cardinal importance. Strood showed his appreciation of its attainment by following McNab's example with the whisky.

"The next thing is your attempt to establish ownership, isn't it, sergeant?" McNab said. "You didn't succeed?"

Strood wiped his lips hastily.

"We haven't yet – no, not quite, for all Hackett's artfulness. You see, sir, after this young Sneyd denied he had lost any case, Hackett takes this one out and asks him to have a closer look at it, holding it out for him to take a hold of. Of course what Hackett was really after was to get him to put his fingers on it so's to get a set of prints that were his for certain. He didn't get 'em, though. Hackett wasn't cute enough that time. Sneyd, he says, first put out his hand as if to take the case, and then drew it back, saying there was no need, as, not having lost his case, he could lay no claim to this one. But, all the same, Hackett noticed one thing; it was his left hand Sneyd put out to take the case with. But Hackett has more than one way to get his prints all right. Sneyd goes a lot to Windygate, where Hackett's girl is parlourmaid. So he's fixed it up with Alice that the next time Sneyd has tea there, which he's been doing quite often, Alice is to get him to handle a plate; and then she'll keep it safe to hand over to Hackett, which will cook his goose, if I'm not mistaken."

McNab said nothing. I recollected his words to me earlier about the cigarette case. He had said Sneyd might be denying ownership for reasons entirely unconnected with Cardew's death. This was less likely now, since it seemed indubitable that the case had been deliberately laid on the road to draw Cardew's attention to it. Further, if it could be proved that these fingerprints were Sneyd's, it became equally certain that Sneyd was the man who had planted it on the road.

McNab ceased drumming the table with his fingers.

"The constable, of course, asked Mr. Sneyd to give an account of his movements between nine and ten o'clock last Wednesday?"

"I did that myself, last night, after having Hackett's report of his interview with Sneyd."

"Well?"

Strood tapped his notebook, to which he had just returned the two fingerprint photographs.

"We're still looking into that. Not satisfactory, so far. Actually, according to his statement, that is, he was in Ashford till about 9.30. Arrived there about 8.30; not to call on anyone – oh, no! – merely to obtain the *Kent Evening Echo* with the latest cricket scores. Having got that, he says he remembered Miss Ann Cardew had gone to London, and so he waited on in the chance of taking her home pillion. But she was not on the 9.13. He then left to go home, got a puncture in his back wheel near Hinckley, tried to do a repair by the roadside, made a mess of it, and then had to wheel the cycle home, which he reached at a quarter to eleven." Strood nodded sagely and went on in a different tone:

"The Ashford newsboy remembers a motorcyclist stopping for a paper, but says it couldn't have been later than eight, because, except on Saturdays, he goes home at that hour. Yes, Sneyd says quite a lot of people met him on the road, but nobody he knew. That's quite likely too, since he's lived here only about two months. We've been trying to find someone who saw him, of course. Hackett's on the job, and knows more or less who's on the road at such times. You see, his alibi amounts to nothing at all, for Burrish itself lies between Bonnington and Hinckley; so that he admits being in the neighbourhood very close to the exact time."

"When are you seeing him again?"

"Tomorrow, at 11.30. I've asked him to see me at the station."

"Mind if we come?"

"Glad, sir. You've quite convinced me that Mr. Robert Sneyd is the man for our money."

"Have I?" He gazed over thoughtfully at the burly officer. "Don't be so sure, Strood, my friend." And when Strood stared back at him he rose. "You see, I haven't been able to convince myself – as yet," he added.

Strood bent to pick up his cap, and then got to his feet, stretching himself. He seemed quite satisfied.

"You forget you're in the country, sir. Up in London there's maybe, in a manner of speaking, a thousand or two possible suspects to every case. Here it's easier for us. And in this particular affair there's simply nobody else but this fellow Sneyd, as far as I can see."

"As far as any of us can see – that's true!" McNab admitted.

It was nearly one when Sergeant Strood slipped away from the Woolpack.

Chapter 10

Next morning we set off to keep our appointment with Strood at the New Romney police station. It was a fine Sunday morning, and the usual Sunday devotions or diversions engaged the attention of the villagers. Here a man in a doorway, and in shirt-sleeves, stood in solemn meditation while he smoked; further on a man bent over a pigsty in an attitude of reverence, kneeling, as it were, on his elbows, to contemplate the occupant. We walked with an air of determination, as of men going to church.

Outside the police station, when we reached it, we saw a motorcycle standing against the wall. Mr. Sneyd, it seemed, had already arrived. McNab halted to look at the cycle. He looked at it quite a time with, it amused me to notice, much the same expression of appreciative rapture that I had seen on the face of the labourer looking at his pig. But McNab had an idea. The next moment he was on his knees beside that cycle. With a twist, off came the magneto cap, while his other hand extracted from his pocket the little packet of rice paper he used for his cigarettes. With the speed of a conjurer he had torn off a minute fragment of paper, inserted it between the platinum points and the contact breaker, and replaced the cap before I well knew what his game was.

Whether that cycle had made him change his plans or not I do not know, but, tearing a leaf from his notebook he scribbled a rather long note and gave it to me, telling me to go in, hand it to Strood, and stay with him. Apparently, as at the inquest, he himself intended to keep in the background. From my previous visit I knew where the office was and, with a knock, entered the room.

How far the interrogation of Sneyd had gone I could not tell, but a look at his face while the sergeant was deciphering McNab's scrawl seemed to show it had gone far, and had not been found very palatable. Sneyd's face had, in fact, a set, cold, hard, defiant expression that bore witness to the thoroughness with which Strood and Hackett were putting him through the mill. But if there was recognition there was no trace of funk in the unamiable glance he cast at me as I took a chair by the window. He went on with a reply to some question apparently put just as I entered.

"Why did I come round by Bonnington and Hinckley? 'Pon my word, I can't say. I just did."

Not till the sergeant had read McNab's note did he look up.

"You have no more satisfactory reason for taking so round-about a way home?"

"None, except that I'd so often taken the other way."

"Did you call at Windygate in passing?"

"I did not."

"Nor at Redcotes?"

"I didn't pass Redcotes, as you know."

"You go quite often to both houses, don't you?"

"Certainly."

"You go and come at all hours?"

"At all reasonable hours. I am on that footing at both places."

"So you will know the road quite well?"

Sneyd looked up with a weary smile.

"Oh, yes, I know what comes next; if I know it so well why did I take it from Ashford."

"Well, why did you"

"The answer is the same, sergeant; I wasn't pressed for time that night."

"That's not the same. Your first answer was that it was less familiar than the direct road."

"Oh, Lord, man, what does it matter?" Sneyd burst out. "The choice of one way or another is often decided by the mood of the moment, and one forgets after taking it what moved one to take it."

He was feeling thoroughly badgered; but Strood was persistent.

"Could you not have also forgotten you turned into the Redcotes road?"

"No. One can forget *why* one took this or that road, but not that one had been actually on that road."

"H'm. I was just wondering if we couldn't find a solution," Strood said thoughtfully. "Now, about that puncture. You say you tried a roadside repair near Hinckley. Did you have a cigarette while busy with your attempt?"

"Can't remember; but it's quite probable."

"Supposing you did, wasn't it possible that in your anxiety to get home you left your case behind, and that someone picked it up and, in their turn, dropped it accidentally on that stretch of road near Redcotes?"

Sneyd's eyes narrowed for a moment.

"Quite impossible, for I did not lose my case."

He spoke quickly, as if to make up for the pause between the question and the reply – a pause unnecessary if the reply were true, I thought. "What day was it you lost your case, then?"

"I haven't lost it at all, I tell you."

"Very good, then you can let us see it?"

"Certainly, but I've left it at home. I can get it inside ten minutes."

"That will be quite satisfactory, Mr. Sneyd," Strood waved a dismissing hand. "We'll await your return."

But that was what we did not do, though we did sit still while we heard Sneyd busy with the kick-starter of his machine. No explosion came – except verbal ones from Sneyd himself. Presently the door was flung open and he put his head inside:

"Bike won't fire. I'll have to hoof it all the way there and back."

But he couldn't have been more than halfway along the tree-bordered road that connects New Romney with Littlestone before his cycle was inside the office, and its back tyre off, McNab meanwhile having procured the tools at a neighbouring garage. But, for once, Sneyd was in luck: there were just two punctures on the tube. I indicated the one, near the valve, on which he had been at work when I first saw him on the Friday; the other puncture, which he alleged he had got on the Wednesday, was far older. McNab pointed out, indeed, that while on the Friday patch the embossed name of the rubber company stood out in bold relief, that on the alleged Wednesday puncture was pressed in flat to the surface. So, though it was obvious to the eye of any experienced motorist that Sneyd had lied when he said he walked home last Wednesday because of a puncture, we could not convict him of it. The tube did show two punctures, the one I had seen him mend, and as for the other, its date was, after all, a matter of opinion.

Hackett alone did not seem much disappointed. He was more anxious to see the cigarette case. He did not doubt Sneyd would return with one. Nor did he care whether it was a borrowed or recently bought cigarette case so long as Sneyd had handled it, as he triumphantly pointed out to us. But here again our luck was out. For when the young man came back it was to produce the sort of case which could no more carry fingerprints than the felt handlebars of his cycle – a case made of figured, coloured and embossed Florentine leather. Hackett's face became a study as he took it in his palm and looked down at it. His jaw just dropped. Sneyd smiled at him. The sergeant's face expressed nothing, but his feelings, I think, were mixed.

Instantly Sneyd seized on the changed situation, as was evident from the alteration in his tone:

"So that's that," he remarked. "Now I hope you're satisfied. For I may tell you I'm now going to act on the advice I'd had about all this, and I've got to tell you that, having out of politeness replied to all reasonable questions, I'm not going to be badgered by any of you any more. Unless and until – rotten phrase that – unless and until you like to bring some definite charge against me."

"And that, of course, they can't do," was McNab's comment when I rejoined him at the garage where he had gone to return the garage man's tools.

"Strood is sure he, at least, knows more than he will tell."

McNab went on washing his oily hands.

"I shouldn't wonder. But he won't tell, and they can't make him. Anything else?"

"Strood is still certain he is actually concerned in Cardew's death."

McNab laughed as he pulled the towel.

"Look now, suppose Hackett gets those fingerprints he's after, and suppose they correspond with those he's already got – what then? He will only succeed in proving that Sneyd was lying when he said he hadn't been on that particular stretch of road that night. As for Mr. Cardew stooping to look at the case planted in the road, Wouldn't you have done the same?"

"Yes, but I'd have picked it up."

"Would you, if in stooping you had a sudden attack of *angina pectoris* which set you staggering?"

"Well, what are you yourself going to do?"

"Allow Strood and his young subordinate to concentrate on Sneyd. That will keep them busy, draw any attention there may be, and distract it from me. In this sort of angling, ye see, it's no bad thing to have a shadow on the waters, provided it's at the wrong spot."

The Sunday afternoon we passed in the Woolpack parlour. A Sunday quiet hung over the place, and all Burrish, after its Sunday dinner, appeared to have sunk into slumber. My own eyelids, indeed, began to feel heavy as I squatted in the armchair and watched McNab busy at the table. His pencil was at work on a notebook, and he had all the scraps of newspaper gleaned yesterday from the dyke neatly arranged at his left hand. Of course he was trying from their separate age, contents and condition to make something out of them. I had myself examined them all. Most had obviously lain among the reeds for months; some had been glued together by moisture, two were washed-out scraps of a private letter, one was a patent medicine puff, another part of a list of stock exchange prices, another half a cricket score in some match, and so on. One might, I thought, just as well have hunted among the Bank Holiday litter left on Hampstead Heath to discover who murdered the Babes in the Wood.

I saw McNab pick up the piece of blue velvet with the rubber band. No wonder he frowned and stared at that! A bit of colour decoration to fasten to a button on a child's frock, it indeed might have had significance as to who murdered the Babes in the Wood, but could hardly have any traceable connection with Mr. Cardew's death.

And yet, now that he had discounted Sneyd and his cigarette case, all he had got to work on lay there before him on the table. That McNab considered the cigarette case of no relevancy I did not, of course, believe. That matter certainly had to be cleared up; but I think he considered it safe in the hands of Strood and Hackett, especially Hackett, while he himself made a direct attempt to get in at once on the man he believed to be behind Sneyd. His argument, I now know, was that, if Strood were right about Sneyd and he himself wrong, then his own investigations must lead back to Sneyd, who would then find himself being approached from two sides.

McNab's dark head bending over the table gradually lost distinctness, the clean-cut, pale face became a blur as my eyes lost focus, and my mind ceased to function...

Ultimately a tapping on the door roused me, and I was in time to see the little girl, Mary, put one half of her face shyly round the edge of the door. Her gaze rested on me doubtfully. McNab laid down his pencil.

"Hullo, Mary, this is nice of you. Come in," he said with great heartiness. Probably he thought any diversion from his present almost hopeless job welcome.

The girl advanced slowly, watching me all the time. Tucked under her arm she carried a big, square book with a gaudy blue cover.

"Mother sent you to keep us company, eh?"

She shook her head.

"Mother's asleep upstairs. So is Ben." She added as an afterthought, "You can hear Ben sleeping."

Then she gently lifted the book on to the table, and, as McNab drew it towards him, she climbed into a chair at his side.

"Oh, a scrapbook!" he cried with affected delight.

"It's got pictures in it."

I closed my eyes again, After that their voices came in whispers.

Much later the loud squeaking of Ben's Sunday boots descending the stairs awakened me. McNab was alone at his papers again. He turned at my yawn.

"Developing country habits and customs quickly, aren't you?" he said.

"Your lady friend gone already?" I retorted.

He laughed in a way that made me get up. I knew that kind of laugh from him. There was a success in it, something had come, he had discovered something.

"She left me her scrapbook, though," he remarked as I stood over him.

"But that's not why you laugh. Child as you are, you aren't so keen on childish pictures as all that," I asserted.

"On some of them I am," he declared. And then, as I seized the book and began to turn its pages, covered with silly, shiny posies of flowers, and gummy rosy garlands, surrounding cigarette cards, prints from the papers, picture postcards, he went on: "Who was it that talked about wasting time? Don't you see, Mr. Chance, in return for my showing her the pictures in *Alice* she comes here to show me her pictures, and puts into my hand something I've wanted so badly, and didn't see how to come by. Yes, sir, at the very moment my head was aching to know how to get it, that child walks in and simply shoves the thing into my hands."

"Now what in Heaven's name are you talking about?" I demanded.

He flung over several of the stiff pages.

"Look at that," he said, stopping at a highly-decorated page. In the centre, surrounded by wreaths of red roses, appeared the picture of a wedding group, cut from some newspaper. Underneath the picture were the words: *Famous Kent Cricketer's Daughter Weds*. Flanking this square central print were two oval pictures, one of the bride and bridesmaids, the other the bridegroom and the best man. McNab laid his finger on this last:

"You recognise them?"

"Yes, they are the two Campbells."

"Fine! That was what I wanted. Good likenesses?"

"Quite, except that Percy, the elder, doesn't wear so heavy a moustache now. This must have been taken a few years back, to judge by the females. But what's the point?"

"Oh, it just makes a start in my investigations.

The photographer, I see, is Singletone, Rye."

This was startling.

"Mac, you surely don't suspect Campbell?" I protested. But I might have known it. Hadn't I said so to myself, yesterday, when he revealed such a prejudice against the two brothers as Anglicised fellow-countrymen of his own!

"N – o," he replied, "no, I don't suspect them, not more than anyone else. It's only that experience has taught me in a case of this sort to distrust all who can show a very strong alibi. I'm simply going to test it, as I'll go on to test that of everyone connected with the affair, till I land on one that breaks down. That's the drab, routine line we must follow in this case."

"You might as well suspect Matheson," I blurted out.

"And so I would," he retorted, "if Matheson stood to gain by Cardew's death."

He sat peering at the cutting with his pocket lens.

Chapter 11

McNab left early on the Monday morning for Rye. It was his intention, after having procured from the photographer there the best possible portraits of the two Campbells, to take the first train to town and go to the hotel in Howard Street, and settle beyond question whether the two had been there on the night of Cardew's death.

But it was not his intention to leave me kicking my heels in idleness during his absence. He had, in fact, left me for the afternoon one piece of work to which I did not look forward at all. This was to call at Redcotes, and if possible get to Ann Cardew, let her see the blue velvet ribbon, and find out if she could make anything of it. At the same time I was to ascertain if her father had been in the habit of carrying a light when he went upstairs to bed.

This mission, I took it, was the result of his long cogitations at the table on the Sunday afternoon. And they were both points on which he wanted immediate information. At the same time I was, if opportunity offered, to get some notion as to the footing on which Robert Sneyd and the man Rowland Todd stood in relation to the various members of the Redcotes family. This last, McNab warned me, was a matter which would call for delicate handling. That, I thought, I could bring to the interview. What I least liked was the notion of solemnly and secretly bringing out that blue velvet trifle which McNab entrusted to me with as many warnings as to its safety as if it had been a pearl of price.

So I happened to be in rather a, not sulky, but contrary mood when, in the early forenoon P.C. Hackett was shown in. His appearance there, at that time, made all the precautions taken by Strood to avoid being seen with us quite futile. The young constable, abashed, no doubt, by the raised eyebrows with which I greeted him, asked nervously if he might see McNab. His face fell when I told him McNab was away for the day. There was a point of procedure on which he was most anxious to secure McNab's opinion. He had been on the telephone on another matter yesterday, and had, he said, heard from a colleague at county headquarters that McNab was rather clever in some ways.

This naive understatement somehow restored my humour. As I listened I made a mental note to tell McNab the zealous Hackett had been inquiring into his past, and had learned that in some ways he was quite clever – and, presumably, in others, not! Hackett, seeing my smile, became confidential.

"It's like this, sir. Up till now, though I've had no big case, I've had some that were puzzles to us. Cases, you understand, that were not to be solved by routine, that needed – well—" He paused, hunting for a word.

"Imagination," I hazarded.

"That's the word – imagination. That's just where books come in – books on crime, I mean."

"But you can have little crime on the Marsh?"

"Not much," he replied, quite regretfully as I observed. "No, not much; but what there is is usually a problem. On account of the loneliness, you see, there's seldom any witnesses to be got."

"No witnesses in the Cardew case, either," I said.

"No, that's a sure thing," Hackett nodded. "That's near the point I wanted to discuss. You see" – he hesitated, readjusting his helmet on his knees – "you see, I've nobody here to discuss things with. The sergeant, a great man in a rough and tumble affair, takes no interest in problems. Now what I've learned to do whenever a problem comes up – a larceny or misdemeanour with no witnesses I mean – is to ask myself three questions: *How? Why? Who?*"

"Well, every crime without witnesses is a problem, whether it be a chicken theft or a murder."

Hackett slapped his leg.

"Exactly! And the chicken theft may be the tougher problem to solve," he said. "But now, sir, if you notice my three questions you will see they lead on, step by step, the first the easiest."

"From the circumference to the centre. Yes, the method is usually self-evident, and the motive usually just less so."

"That's it – exactly like a book! Well, you will notice the difference in the Cardew affair; we're quite certain who did it, we're fairly certain why he did it, but how it was done is beyond us."

This made me sit up – what was new in it, at least. Had Hackett really been able to establish a sufficient motive for murder? And against that man Sneyd? If he had, it must alter McNab's theory that, though Sneyd knew more than he would tell, he was not the actual criminal. I thought rapidly for a few moments, while the young constable brooded over the difficulty of this particular case.

"We agreed just now," I said, "that motive is rather more difficult to establish than method easier to see the knife, or the poker, and so on, than to say why they were used. But strong motives may exist without murder following. For example, Hackett, a man with a strong motive, will not, if he is of a placid or timid nature, seek satisfaction by murder; while another man with a far weaker motive, but of hasty or bitter temper, may do so."

Hackett looked at me approvingly.

"I like talking it over with you," he said ingenuously. "If only the sergeant would talk it over. Not that I'd expect him to talk like a book; but if only he would discuss a problem!" He sat forward. "Now look, sir, it's like this. We know the people on the Marsh, and we know what they thought of Mr. Cardew. He hadn't an enemy. No one had a grudge against him. We'd have heard plenty about it if anybody had. They're not exactly tongue-tied on the Marsh; and they haven't a lot to talk about. But round Burrish there's been lots of talk about this fellow Sneyd. You heard him tell us he was on a friendly footing at both Redcotes and Windygate, went and came as he liked? We knew better. Windygate maybe, but not Redcotes. Before he went to India—"

"India?"

"Well, Ceylon, I believe 'twas. Some three years back, there was trouble between Mr. Cardew and him on account of Miss Ann. I've got witnesses who will swear to hearing high words between the two men at the time. Young Sneyd, you see, had come to Redcotes as assistant – same job as Mr, Rowland Todd has now – and there was trouble over his attentions to the young miss. Sneyd gets sacked, and then goes off tea-planting, or rubber growing, in Ceylon. And no more trouble till he turns up on six months' leave – to begin his tricks again. That's the story. As for the example you mentioned, well, you saw *his* temper yesterday – neither sweet-tempered nor timid, I'm sure."

In this I agreed with Hackett; Sneyd was certainly not timid, and as for his temper, I had, besides yesterday, the clear-cut memory of the first time I had seen him, when Ann Cardew ducked and ran like a hare because she did not wish to be seen.

"Well," I admitted, "you do seem to have fairly found answers to the *Why* and the *Who* of the case."

"But, so far, nothing towards answering the flow."

"And that is essential."

Hackett rose.

"Here it looks like it. We must know how he did it if we are to clinch the thing on to him. My opinion is that the confidence you saw him show yesterday rests on his belief that we'll never find out."

"Well," I said, rising too, "we'll see about that. Never's a long time, Hackett."

"Has your friend hit on any theory yet, about how it was done?" he inquired.

"Not yet – not to me, anyhow."

His face fell. So that was why he had paid us his visit. Another mental note I made was to tell McNab that Hackett had come to pick his brains.

But I had not nearly exhausted the thoughts the enthusiastic young constable roused before I reached Redcotes. McNab had told me Miss Ann was prepared for anyone he might send, and would not be surprised at my visit. Even so what I had learned from Hackett, apart from a visit in the household's present circumstances, was quite enough to make me feel uncomfortable.

The house was a fine Georgian structure, of the grave dignity characteristic of its period. As I walked round the half drive beside that sand-dressed lawn – which, as Hackett had told me, bore no footprints save those of Mr. Cardew, Jippling and the other man who had assisted in carrying the victim into the house – I felt that everyone of its many windows was an eye, watching my approach with cold disfavour. But this, as it turned out, was much the worst moment I experienced.

The room into which I was shown contained a few people quietly talking together while having tea. Ann Cardew, teacup in hand, advanced to meet me. She was smiling as I took her extended hand; an evanescent smile, it is true; but I had not seen her smile at all till then. In her thin black dress she looked more fragile than I had supposed, the dark eyes larger, the lips paler, but, without a hat to hide the nice lines of her head, even more attractive.

After the exchange of the usual commonplaces, she led me over to her aunt at the tea-table. I thought I recognised the moment at which these presumably very intimate friends had arrived. Yes, that made it easier for me. It was the moment when after tragedy the mind seeks to reach out again; when, after shock, life, which must go on, begins to readjust and renew itself.

They need, with me, make no references that came near to what had preoccupied all their minds. The vicar, or at least his wife – a lady with a red face, slack mouth and an ill-considered hat – already knew I was at the Woolpack; also that I was there to write about the Marsh. What she did not know was how I had formed an acquaintance with Miss Ann Cardew. But, if she failed to dispel her ignorance on the spot, it was not because she didn't try.

I recall, too, being approached by a military-looking old gentleman who, having heard my name, asked me over his poised teaspoon if I were any relation to old Charley Chance of the Hampshires. I had no need to be rescued from him. He turned his back on hearing I was neither a relation of old Charley's nor one of the Suffolk Chances. But I did need rescue from Mrs. Shortt, the vicar's wife, and I fancy it was Ann herself who, seeing me so beset, sent Percy Campbell to drag me out of her clutches.

"Care for a cigarette and a look at the garden?" he asked.

His eyes did twinkle at my eager assent. Overeager it must have been, to judge by the lady's sniff. Campbell took my arm till we reached the garden.

"Ann has just been explaining you," he said confidentially, as if we were still within range of Mrs. Shortt's ears.

"Yes," I returned, wondering how much exactly Ann had explained.

"Glad you came," he went on heartily.

Though uncertain whether he referred to that afternoon, or to my presence in Burrish, I liked his frank smile, and the nod accompanying it.

"It's a nice place." My reply covered both Burrish and Redcotes.

"Oh, you know what I mean. You're the man she consulted in town." He paused, and I had time to note that Ann had not told him all. She did seem capable of acting on McNab's instructions, whatever they were. "Well, her instinct was right. I do hope you'll be able to help us, Mr. Chance. For it's obvious, isn't it, that things can't be left as they are, after all the talk there's been?"

"Quite so."

He looked over at Rowland Todd, who also emerged, with Dr. Cyril Campbell.

"It's got to be probed to the depths, as my brother puts it."

"You have no theory yourself?" I inquired.

"As to that, it was what I was going to ask you," he said. He shook his head. "No, none of us have. And you, I take it, have so far developed no theory?"

"I have nothing to say as yet." Then, as the others began to file out, I thought a warning opportune. "If you haven't already done so, may I beg you to say nothing to anyone as to why I am here?"

With great frankness he gave me this most necessary assurance.

"I haven't, and I won't. No one guesses, except my brother Cyril, and he, of course, doesn't count. As a medical man he knows how to keep his mouth shut, but, as he'll tell you himself, at that I can give him points."

Then others joined us, but Ann carried me off to see some flowers at the end of the garden. We came to rest on a bench amid a clump of evergreen oaks. It was dread of getting hunted down by the vicar's wife that made me go straight to the matters on which McNab had sent me there. I simply produced the blue velvet thing.

"Can you tell me anything about that?" I asked.

Astonishment came to the eyes I watched. She bent forward to look.

"No, I've never seen it before. Does it mean anything?" she added quickly, turning to me.

"That's what we want to know. You are sure you can say nothing about it – not what it is meant for, nor where it comes from, or who had it, or anything like that?"

She took it in her hand, turned it over, and shook her head.

"You can't connect it in any way with what – what happened? It was picked up near the place."

She gave a little cry as she understood to what I referred, and her eyes, which had been fastened on me, dilated in a fixity of horror. I was about to repeat my previous question when two moving shadows crossed the grass at my feet. Looking up, I saw Dr. Campbell and Todd slowly strolling past us. The poor girl was, I am sure, oblivious of their presence. I placed my hand over the piece of ribbon, and, as I did so, was aware of a sudden pause in the flow of conversation between the two men. To them it must have seemed, if they were looking, that I had momentarily taken hold of Miss Cardew's hand. But better that than that they should see what her hand held.

Ann Cardew shook her head again.

"No, certainly I've never seen that before, It must be just an accident that – that—"

"Quite. Dropped by some child, probably. Forget about it."

"Is that all you've found?" she asked.

"Yes, but I've something else to ask you, though. It's about something you told us in London."

A quick shiver as of pain went like a wave across her face.

"Yes," she said. "Go on."

"It was about your father's looking through the staircase window." I hurried over it. "I have to ask you if he was in the habit of carrying a light when he went upstairs?"

"He used to," she replied. "But he had done without a light for some time before I first saw him at the window."

"Do you know why?"

"I was quite sure it was so that he might see what was outside."

"Thank you; that's all."

But she did not rise as I expected. She sat looking down at the slender hand which was smoothing imaginary creases in her dress. And very white the hand looked against the black frock.

"There's one thing," she said tentatively.

"Yes?"

"Everyone will soon know why you are in Burrish."

"How soon?"

"Well, a few days. You can't hide much in the country. Percy saw you at the – in the schoolroom, and guessed at once."

"But your brother-in-law is rather exceptional, isn't he? I mean the average level of intelligence doesn't reach his level."

The pale ghost of a smile moved her lips.

"No," she admitted. "And even he has got you mixed up – I mean he thinks you are the big man from London."

"And you left him to think so?

"Acting under instructions."

Her last words came in a hurried whisper. And as I got up I found that young Todd and the doctor were about to pass us on their second circuit of the garden. Only, this time, they did not pass, and Ann introduced me. Cyril Campbell smiled – he had a nice, frank smile, and, like his brother, good eyes. Unlike his brother, his hair was close cropped, in a soldierly way. He seemed thinner and slighter also; an effect which he probably owed to his infinitely better-cut clothes.

"Heard quite a lot about you through Mrs. Shortt," he said, holding out his hand.

"Through Mrs. Shortt?" I echoed, uncomprehending.

"Your answers to her catechism, I mean."

"Then you should have said 'overheard,' Cyril," Todd remarked, flicking the ash of his cigarette over a flower. He did not offer his hand. Todd I did not take to at all. Younger than both the Campbells as he was, his rather lined face, sharp nose, and almost lipless mouth made him seem older.

"Believe you've come down to write up the Marsh," he said. "Papers like that sort of picturesque stuff now – the Discovery of Unknown England, eh? Well, don't glorify us too much. We have our defects just as much as Wigan or Bootle."

His eyes wandered after Ann Cardew as she went towards Colonel Glidden and his daughter, who had got stranded. But Campbell's eyes were on Todd, rather intently, I thought.

"I'll undertake not to overlook the defects," I said dryly.

"Eh?" Todd came back to attention.

"What I write won't be a catalogue of your virtues."

He laughed.

"That's right. Nothing so dull as virtues."

"Except vices," Campbell said quietly.

Todd turned on him.

"Well, old man, I admit you ought to know about that."

Campbell took his arm.

"Let's go and put it to the vicar's wife," he said with mock earnestness.

That was enough to send me off! I made for the house to find my hat, and there ran across the elder Campbell. He, in the absence of any host, appeared to be doing the honours of the house.

Anyway, he saw me off.

"Come over and see us at Windygate," he said, pressing my hand. "I might be able to help, you know. Anyhow, I'm there to consult whenever you wish."

On reaching the Woolpack I found McNab waiting for me. He seemed worried.

Chapter 12

"Well, what's happened?" I asked. "Does this mean you have no progress to report?"

"It simply means that I got through the job quicker than I expected. Sit down; I'll tell you all the facts, though I'm not pretending they can be explained – by me, anyway."

When I had plunged into the armchair, he dragged over a chair for himself, and then sat it a-straddle, facing the back – a favourite attitude when about to expound a case or a situation.

"This I can tell you at once," he began, "the Campbells are cleared of suspicion."

"Never had any suspicion myself. Is that why you look unhappy?"

Up went his hand at my interruption; and the gesture, coming over the back of the chair, reminded me of a man in a pulpit. He had not, apparently, forgotten my assertion that he was biased against the brothers because they were Anglicised fellow-countrymen of his own.

"One other such word," he said sternly, "and you hear no more."

It was a horrible threat. I collapsed.

"Go on, I'll try to be helpful."

"That Rye photographer is a good man. I am not referring to his morals, but to his habits, which are business-like. He files all his negatives. But I had to be content with the print of the bridegroom and the best man which he made me from the old negative. From Rye I got to town by the 1.30 and went at once to Romeike and Curtice with my scraps of newspapers, to know if they could identify the papers, and assign a date to each. I had intended, you see, to leave the eight pieces with them to get to work on, and call back for results after having been to settle matters at the hotel. The manager, however, said it was possible they might be able to identify the papers in a few minutes if I cared to wait. I had known, of course, that much might be done by one of their experts, familiar with all sorts of newspapers; but I hadn't known just how much there is to go on, colour and quality of paper, difference in type, ink, spacing, width of column, and so on. Every man to his own job! And on this job the office got pretty keen."

McNab felt for his notecase. "I'll not bother you with the separate identifications; but it's a wonder how some of those scraps should have come to rest in a Romney Marsh ditch; for one was from the *Plymouth News*, another the *Manchester Guardian*, another the *Times*; the next identified was a trade paper, *Poultry Keeping*, then followed the *Kent Evening Echo*; and the last three were the *Live Stock Journal*, *Church Times* and *Scotsman*. A queer assortment! One would hardly have expected to find the *Scotsman* at the bottom of a ditch in Kent – eh?"

It was too much to resist this opening.

"Oh, I don't know. Dante is said to have found a Scotsman in hell, you know."

"I do know – Michael Scott by name; and by profession he was exactly what I'd need to be to get much further in this case," he said ruefully.

"What was he?"

"A wizard."

He slipped a wedge-shaped scrap of newspaper from the notecase and handed it over to me.

"Look at that!" he said.

On one side was a small section of a large display advertisement; the other gave part of the score in a county cricket match. I had seen this the day before, when he was pondering over all the slips arranged on the table, and had then noticed that this one, besides being the smallest, was also much the freshest in condition.

"They are all trifles," he resumed. "Heaven alone could know what are the odds against any one of them having a connection with the case. But when one has nothing else, one begins on anything; and I hadn't forgotten what that blade of grass did in the case you know of. Well, after identification, the next job was to 'date' them. This could be done to a certainty, of course, but not speedily enough for me. Except the one in your hand, which is from the *Kent Evening Echo*. Just look at it again: it tells its own date and even the time of issue.

```
and his hitting brought on Durston at 212.

           Kent—1st Innings
Ashdown, c Cutmore, b Holmes........    4
J. L. Bryan, b Durston...............   18
Woolley, c Holmes, b Newman..........  125
Ames, b Holmes.......................   41
T. C. Longfield, c Bettington, b New-
    man..............................    9
T. F. Mitchell, not out..............   42
                                      ----
       Total, 5 wkts.................  239
```

"When the news-cutting expert identified that as coming from the *Kent Evening Echo* I at once got through on the phone to the office in Folkestone. From there I learned not only that the fragment we had identified came from the issue of the previous Wednesday, but also that the state of the score showed it to be from the final edition, which is issued in Folkestone at 5.15, and which would reach Ashford approximately about three-quarters of an hour later."

"So this bit of paper must have gone into the dyke at or about the time Cardew met his death? That looks as if Sneyd spoke the truth when he said he had gone to Ashford to get the paper."

"Sneyd," McNab said impressively, "has not, so far, in any single instance been *proved* to have spoken anything but the truth."

"But it does not tally with his assertion that he had not been on the Redcotes road," I objected.

McNab took the scrap of newspaper between his fingers.

"Little wind it would need to blow this from where he admits he was to where I found it trapped in the ditch."

"But you don't know there was any wind that night."

"I do – at sunset, for half an hour, there were intermittent gusts from the south-east. Wind from that quarter is rare locally, and this, with the phenomenal heat, made people remember the fact, as it seemed at the time to portend a break in the weather."

"But, McNab, a breeze from the south-east would have blown it in the opposite direction."

"Quite true," he admitted frankly.

"Besides, at sunset this edition of the paper had hardly reached Ashford."

"That also is true. But what then?"

"What then? Why, surely that disposes of the absurd suggestion that this scrap of the newspaper Sneyd bought at Ashford was blown by a wind that didn't exist at the time he bought it to the spot you found it; it proves you are wrong, anyway."

"It does nothing of the sort. If it proves anything it proves that this scrap does not come from the copy Sneyd bought at Ashford. You forget that while admittedly Sneyd passed along the Windygate road at about 9.15 on Wednesday night, I found the paper in the ditch about one o'clock on Saturday last. What is there to show when, between these two times, this rag of paper went into the dyke? As for absurdity, does it not strike you as equally absurd to visualise Sneyd dismounting somewhere between Windygate and Burrish to tear a scrap from his newspaper?"

"Put like that, it does," I conceded.

"Precisely. But, so far, I see no other way to put it," he muttered, as with a sigh he slipped the paper back into his pocket.

For myself, I could not help feeling that, when taken in conjunction with the cigarette case, the overwhelming probability was that the paper scrap had a connection with Sneyd's presence on the Redcotes road that night. I was certain we had not yet finished with the bit of paper. So it surprised me when McNab, leaning both arms along the back of the chair, said, as if he had read my thought:

"But we are finished with the Campbells. That is something. There is not the least doubt about them."

"I'm sure you wouldn't leave them the smallest loophole," I said, for it seemed to me that he was as much prejudiced against the brothers as he was prejudiced in favour of Sneyd.

A smile broke out on his perplexed face.

"Right, Godfrey. I went very minutely into the Campbell alibi. The Massacre of Glencoe was responsible for that."

"The what?" I cried, astounded.

"Don't tell me you never heard of it – the killing of the MacDonalds by Campbell of Breadalbane in Glencoe?" he demanded incredulously.

"Well, now you mention it, I seem to remember something in the *Record* about it at the time."

"Innisbuie! What a memory; it happened in 1689."

This annoyed me. I had been thinking of some other crime.

"Oh, all right. But what has the Massacre of Glencoe to do with your investigations at the Norfolk Hotel?"

"It was responsible for the very great care I took at the hotel. You see, Chance, that event in Glencoe, and a good many others, got the Campbells a bad name in Scotland. Campbell is a name suspect to this day. So much so that the first thought of any old Scot's wife who had mislaid her specs would be to ask if anybody of the name of Campbell had been seen near the house. Not, mind you," he added, "that it's a principle on which the Scottish police act when investigating a crime."

"But you acted on it."

He smiled.

"*The fathers have eaten sour grapes and the children's teeth are set on edge*. If your name had been McNab you would know why. The sins of the fathers over again. For doubtless there are many kind and honest Campbells in the world now. Anyway, I was not long at the Norfolk Hotel before I became satisfied there were at least two."

"Sure you left no stone unturned?" I maliciously inquired.

There were times when I liked Francis McNab the better through discovering a weakness in him. Then I felt less his inferior. These weaknesses in him were invariably racial. Here in this case, for example, I saw from the moment the Campbell brothers were mentioned that I must be on my guard to save McNab from fastening the crime upon them. What a man he would have been if only he had been an Englishman!

"Not one stone unturned, you may be sure. I inspected the register, and found their signatures. They had occupied rooms 28 and 29 on the second floor. I pulled out the photographs and they were at once recognised by the lady clerk. Besides, the two men were known at the hotel, having stayed there, together and separately, quite frequently. But I went further. I asked to see the restaurant books, and found that numbers 28 and 29 were both charged for dinner and breakfast. Then the chambermaid was sent for, and on being shown the photos at once supplied the names. The girl, in fact, laughed when she saw the younger brother's face, recalling to the manageress the fuss Dr. Campbell had made about the absence of a hot water bottle from his bed. Warm as the weather was, he had explained that, having been so long in India, and having also suffered from malaria, he must have extra warmth. The manageress instantly remembered this incident.

"'They are both rather – well, exigent,' she said, turning to me with a smile of recollection. 'The other gentleman – the one with the auburn hair – telephoned down to complain that his shoes had not been properly polished, and afterwards he put his foot beside the other's to show that even then they were not as well done.'"

That I had been right about the Campbells gratified me so much that I couldn't help rallying McNab on his abortive visit.

"Sure there's no loophole?" I said. "Couldn't one of them have slipped out and been away all night?"

But McNab frankly admitted his failure.

"No," he said, "even if both had been away all night and got back in the morning that would prove nothing. For both were seen in the hotel by the clerk, the porter and two chambermaids round about a quarter to ten, and James Cardew, beyond all question, was dead at ten. That, by itself, is conclusive: the two Campbells have an alibi which is what it appears to be."

Later, after dinner that night, when Mrs. Beddoes had withdrawn, he began to question me about my visit to Redcotes. As it seemed the right moment, I let him know what Hackett had said as to the strength of their case against Sneyd. When I had finished he appeared a little shaken. So at least I thought. He was disturbed on hearing that the police had evidence of a quarrel between Sneyd and Mr. Cardew.

"It looks black," he said; "but, you know, you can build up a case against almost anyone."

This seemed mere perversity, as I told him at once. To accuse McNab, the logician, of perversity, was equivalent to accusing a bishop of bigamy. And, not to my surprise, in the name of logic he repudiated the charge.

"You say Sneyd is a quarrelsome fellow?" he began pugnaciously.

"Certainly. Of that I had first-hand evidence."

"Do you say Mr. Cardew was quarrelsome?"

"On the contrary, he was known to all as the most kindly man on the Marsh."

"But he quarrelled with Sneyd."

"Admitted."

"Was he the only person with whom Sneyd quarrelled?"

"Probably not."

"But he was the only one who suffered fatally in the quarrel – the most kindly man in the district, and therefore the least provocative! Why?"

"His daughter, Ann – you forget."

"Come, come, would his daughter Ann not then have known of whom her father went in fear? If she did know, what was the point of her visit to us?"

As the memory of that visit returned, and I saw again Ann Cardew as she was that night, above all in her despair, I said:

"No, she did not know, and could not even guess at his trouble."

McNab rose and banged his fist on the table.

"That's the truth, Godfrey! She could not guess at the cause. But," he added bitterly, "we did the guessing for her – and guessed wrong." He stood a moment looking down gloomily at the tobacco he was stuffing into his pipe. Not till he had seated himself, with both arms folded on the table and his pipe lit, did he look across at me. "One of your chief uses, Godfrey," he said in a lighter tone, "is that you so often take it upon yourself to act as devil's advocate. It is most helpful. You force me to clarify and purge my thinking processes. Some of the results you've just had. But here are two more points you had better note about this man Sneyd. The first point is that a crime of anger, as this is said to be, is swift, fierce and sudden; it is not a crime planned in the deliberate, methodical, cold-blooded manner in which James Cardew was done to death. The other point is that due allowance must be made for the limitations of the local police. A localised police force is too apt to be unduly impressed by local people, especially by people of some social position. They are also apt to be unduly suspicious of people unknown to them. That was why Hackett told you there wasn't anyone else to suspect but Sneyd. There are a great multitude like Hackett. They think they can forecast the behaviour of people they know. More often than not they are right. For they have seen these people, year in, year out, following a routine life that never varies. But what they overlook is that with all of us each day's routine is carried out in a different spirit and mood. Actions and habits are simple and easy to read, but the character that lies behind them is complex and hard to read. And sometimes a day comes when the man we thought we knew does something out of character, as we say; and if it is discovered there is a scandal, a noise in the papers, and general amazement. How often, for instance, in your early days on the *Record*, have you heard the magistrate modify a sentence on account of the accused's previous good character? Strictly speaking, all they knew anything about was his previous good habits. And that is all the police here know of the man responsible for Cardew's death. He is a man whose known habits disguise his real character."

The impressiveness with which he spoke was not lost on me. If he were right, the man would be hard to get at. And it was when I felt this that I remembered and told McNab of Mr. Campbell's offer of help.

"I suppose we could safely accept his offer now that he himself is cleared?" I said tentatively.

"Certainly," he replied. "Campbell's the very man we need. He knows the neighbourhood."

This looked like progress.

"We can see him tomorrow," I said.

"*You* can see him. I am out of sight, remember. We can make no exception of Campbell. Listen to all he suggests – and tell him nothing."

"Well, it's queer, but he takes me for the man Ann Cardew went to see in London."

"Queer, is it? Surely not, considering all the trouble taken to give that impression."

"Oh, the impression has been taken all right. You are supposed to be simply my friend, and not specially interested. Why, even the vicar's—"

An agitated knocking on the door stopped me. Before either of us spoke, Mrs. Beddoes, opening the door, put a scared face into the room, looking to where I sat.

"Sergeant Strood to see you, sir," she said tremulously.

Two policemen to see me in one day!

The sergeant stepped inside and carefully shut the door. Then, as he turned to us, I saw his face convulsive with excitement. For a moment he seemed to find utterance difficult.

"They've got him!" he whispered hoarsely.

"Got who?" I cried. "The man who killed Cardew?"

But he never looked at me as he replied:

"Got him – Hackett – he's – he's dead."

"But who is he?" I demanded.

McNab stepped forward and took Strood by the arm.

"Poor Hackett," he said quietly.

Chapter 13

No two words I have ever heard came as a greater shock than McNab's two quiet words of pity for the dead young constable. Till I overheard them my thought had been that Hackett had discovered something new, got the man, and thus forestalled McNab. The actual truth stunned me.

"Was it at the same spot?" I heard McNab ask.

"So I understand. The call came from Redcotes. I'm on my way there."

"Right, we'll come too," McNab said.

Strood pulled himself together, but till we were out on the road few words passed. My own thoughts ran on Hackett and the talk I had had with him earlier in the day. Strood was the first to speak.

"Do you think, sir," he said, "that Hackett had got hold of something?"

"That's just what I was thinking," McNab responded. "Looks as if he had got to know too much."

"It's since this forenoon, then," I said to Strood. "He came in anxious to consult about something."

"Said nothing to you?" McNab asked Strood after an interval.

"I've been away all day. But I fancy poor Hackett got hold of something. The message said Jippling had seen a dark object lying at the roadside as he was going home, and when he got closer he found it was Hackett, dead, with his notebook in his hand."

"Ah!"

This exclamation of McNab's held a world of meaning.

"That's what I'm wondering too, sir. I told them to leave the body where it was, and to see that nothing was touched till I came."

"Who rang you up?"

"Mr. Percy Campbell. He said he would see to it that this should be done. Jippling, he added, had just come running to the door, but he himself had not yet seen the body."

In the distance the hooting of a car came across the silent flats, and I turned to see two headlights swing round into the Redcotes road.

"That should be the doctor," Strood said. "He has been prompt."

We stood waiting as the car came rapidly on. Then the sergeant stepped forward into the glare of its headlights, signalling a halt.

"Been very quick, sir," he said as he held the door open for us.

"Happened to be at Brooklands; they phoned me there," the doctor replied as he restarted the car.

After that the two talked in tones too low for us in the back seat to hear what passed. McNab, at my side, said nothing. Over the others' shoulders, ahead of us, I could see a small light on the road that looked like a stationary hand lantern. Strood halted the car some twenty yards or so from the lantern, round which, as we got out, I saw some figures gathered. One of these came forward to meet us. I saw it was Dr. Campbell.

"Yes," he said, "he is dead."

"And the cause?" Dr. Jones inquired.

"Not apparent. But I did not feel justified, in the sergeant's absence, to do more than ascertain that life was extinct."

We went forward. Hackett lay on his back, his head resting on the grass edge of the road, on to which his legs, slightly apart, extended. His left hand, which rested on his chest, still maintained a grip on the notebook. Indeed, for all that appeared to the contrary, he might have seated himself in order to write whatever he had to enter in that book, and then have fallen asleep, his arm bending inward as he sank backwards, so that the notebook came to rest, naturally face downward, on his chest, with the back of his hand uppermost. His right-hand fingers, however, had apparently lost the pencil, although I noticed the finger and thumb were still together as if a pencil were being held. So much was quickly observable, and as I stared down at the body, over which Dr. Jones was now bending, a voice quietly said:

"Nothing has been touched."

Turning, I found Mr. Campbell at my side. He nodded gravely.

"Quite right," I said.

About ten yards further along the light glinted on the handlebars of a push-bike lying at the edge of the road. We all stood watching the doctor, George Jippling holding up the light. Jippling nodded towards the cycle. "I saw that as you come across, sir; it a'nt been moved," he said to Mr. Campbell. Another man, evidently one of the Redcotes stockmen, stared down at the body, his eyes below the uplifted lantern gleaming white with horror. A whispered word or two passed between Strood and McNab. Someone's foot shuffled for a moment on the gritty road. But the doctor's examination did not last long. He rose from his knees.

"That's all now," he said brusquely.

"Shock, you think?" This from Dr. Campbell.

"Shock there's certainly been," he responded, handing back to Strood the flashlight he had used to peer into the dead man's eyes. And then, as we stood silent, no one uttering the one word that was in all our minds, the stillness was rent by the approach of a motorcycle from the Redcotes direction. That was a sound that made me jump, anyhow. A grip took me by the forearm.

"Quiet – you're wrong," McNab breathed in my ear under cover of the noise.

And it was not Sneyd: it was Todd, the Redcotes bailiff, who dismounted gently as soon as he divined something wrong. Afterwards it came out that he had remained in the stockyard later than usual to attend to an ailing heifer. While the situation was being whispered to him by someone Dr. Jones and the sergeant conferred together apart. My own attention was riveted by that notebook in the dead man's hand. What secret might not the hidden page contain? When would they take it from his grasp and read what Hackett had set down? For of course the young officer must have made a discovery, or certainly was well on the way to a discovery. If that were not so, and if the fact were not known to someone who had reason to fear, Hackett would not now be dead. Sergeant Strood raised his voice slightly.

"Now, gentlemen," he said in a tone of quiet authority, "I must ask you to go. All of you I'll see again tomorrow."

Todd was the only one whose way took him through the village, and before he left I heard Strood beg him to say nothing about the event as he passed. Todd, I thought, went reluctantly; but the Campbells seemed to be relieved. They had had enough trouble already.

"Call us if you want help later – about the removal, I mean." Percy Campbell nodded towards the body.

Then we got to work. While the doctor and the sergeant made a search for marks of external violence we stood by, McNab with Strood's flashlight, I with Jippling's storm lantern. It was the notebook that held my eyes all the time.

"Do you think he got anything down?" I whispered. "He has no pencil."

McNab did not reply, so I repeated my question.

"Can't tell," he said; "might have dropped the pencil because he no longer needed it. But look at his grip on the book!"

They soon satisfied themselves that there was no obvious external injury to account for Hackett's death. The doctor rose.

Then Strood, still on his knees, put his hand on the dead man's hand, and with little trouble gently slid the notebook from his fingers. We all looked over Strood's shoulders, and what I read as I held the lantern close to the sergeant's head was this:

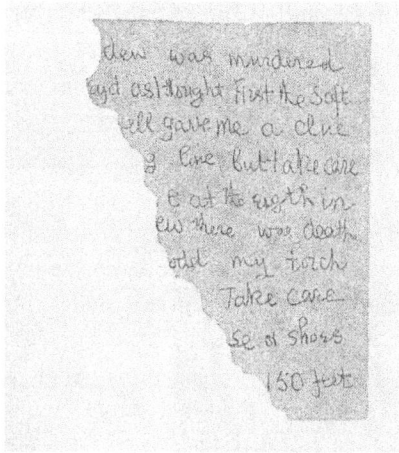

"Someone has got at this *since* he wrote it," Strood declared. The leaf was shaking in his hand.

"Or he may have torn it himself," McNab said. "There is his other hand, you know. What do you think, doctor?"

"Impossible to say what his fingers might do while he passed into unconsciousness. And his hand and wrist were abrased and swollen as if by a fall from his bicycle, as you see."

"If only he still held that pencil we would know some other hand must have torn away this page," Strood muttered.

"Take care of what's left, sergeant. It's not all gone.

There and then we started the search for the missing part of the page torn from the notebook. The night was not quite windless – a draught of air could be felt against one's face at intervals – but even so we had the hope that the paper might have got caught against some roadside tuft of grass...

The half-page we did not find; but Strood came on an electric torch some twenty yards from the body. The cry he gave on finding it brought us to him, for we imagined he had come on what we all were seeking.

"This is Hackett's," he said. A click came. "But it's out of order; it won't light."

Handing over his own torch to me, he examined the other, and, turning up the end, we saw that the screw cap was missing. Strood inserted his finger into the cylinder.

"Hullo, battery's gone," he said. "No wonder it wouldn't light."

"Try your own battery in it," McNab suggested.

I unscrewed the end, and the change was made. Hackett's torch worked perfectly. Then, as Strood flashed it about, I saw something bright on the ground about two yards away. It proved to be the missing cap from the torch. The sergeant was puzzled.

"But where is the battery? That at least can't have been blown away," he said.

We searched the vicinity carefully, with no more success, however, than had so far rewarded our hunt for the missing leaf from the notebook.

"Where exactly did you pick up the torch?" McNab asked.

"Just where you saw me with it in my hand," Strood replied.

"Yes; but the spot – can you show me that?" Strood led us back to the place and, bending down, indicated a tuft of stiff grass about two feet from the road's edge.

"That's the place; it was lying, aslant, in that clump. The bull's-eye end reflecting my light first took my eye, and I—" He broke off. "My God," he breathed – and stopped.

"Yes?" McNab said.

"It's the very spot where Hackett found that little stick stuck in the ground. Look, behind the clump o' grass, there's the stone I put myself to mark the place." He turned appealingly to McNab.

"What do you make of that, sir?"

After a moment the response came:

"Except that it was here both men met their deaths – nothing at all."

"Hackett wanted a light here," said Strood, in the tone of a man trying to puzzle out a perplexing situation. "Hackett, for some reason, wanted to see here. So he took out his torch, and when it would not light he opened the end to see what was wrong. Then he dropped it – eh? Why? And what happened after that?"

"Something that made him want to go back to the point where he had left his cycle," McNab said.

"Yes, and he had left that a good fifty yards down the road. Now, just why had he done that?"

"His cycle lamp may tell us, sergeant."

"His lamp?"

"Yes; it's out now, but if we find it was turned or blown out, and has not merely died out, he probably wanted to come to this spot unseen."

"Yes, I can see that. So he took his torch to get a light at some particular moment?"

"Most probably. But he never got it; and he didn't know why till he examined the torch."

"Which means—"

"Which means that some other hand had previously removed the battery – someone who *knew* he would want to use it, and who didn't want it to be used."

"And then," Strood went on eagerly, "when he finds out what's been done to it, he starts off back for his cycle – to get his lamp, do you think?"

"That we cannot tell yet. But he never got there. He sat down on the grass where we found him and took out his notebook. By that time he knew he was dying. He may have wanted the lamp on his bicycle to see to write. But he couldn't reach it; he had to do what he could where he was."

"In the dark?" Strood ejaculated.

"Certainly," McNab said.

Here was a matter in my own province. And Strood appeared rather incredulous.

"It's fairly easy," I said, "to write on white paper in what for ordinary purposes is darkness. I've often had to write when it was much darker than it is now. All that happens is that you can't keep so straight a line, and probably the writing will be much larger than usual with you."

Strood produced Hackett's notebook. I switched off the torch.

"You see," I said, "you can read it even without a direct light on it. Often I've had to write when I couldn't read what I'd written."

"It's certainly bigger – twice as big as Hackett wrote."

And this was at once evident to us when Strood turned back the pages to the entries of an earlier date.

The examination of the cycle lamp did not take long. Strood unscrewed the burner and, inspecting the well, answered for it that the lamp had not died out for want of oil. And, as on the application of a match the wick developed a good-sized flame, it was safe to say the lamp had been intentionally blown out. With that we had carried the investigation as far as it could be carried there and then.

After giving the necessary assistance to the sergeant and the doctor, who were taking the body on to Jippling's cottage for a more complete examination, we walked back to the Woolpack.

And I well remember that McNab never spoke one word all the way.

Chapter 14

Late as it was, tired as we both were, there was no question of going to bed – not, anyhow, till the case as it now stood had been fully reconsidered. But for nearly two long hours we sat up waiting for Strood. At last we heard the doctor's car stop a little way down the road, and a few moments later I was opening the door for the sergeant. He looked dead beat, and sat down heavily.

"You will understand," he said, "that, after this, the case passes into the hands of the D.D.I."

"You've phoned the Divisional Detective Inspector? What's his name?"

"Rawnsley. He is coming first thing tomorrow."

McNab nodded.

"So the doctor and you found something?"

"No, we found nothing on the body, nothing external to account for death. He thinks it must be poison."

This theory did not, I noticed, take McNab by surprise. At once he shook his head.

"No. I've considered that," he said with finality, "and it's most unlikely. There hasn't been time for it. Hackett discovered something since you saw him this morning, and was acting on it when he met his death. Ever had any experience in poison cases, Strood?"

"Well, no, sir; poison's hardly a way anybody down here would take to. Don't see how they'd get it, either."

"Don't they dip sheep here?"

"Oh, yes. And there's poison in that, you mean?"

"Arsenic. But that's slow and, like most poisons, is followed by symptoms. And, like all poisons, has to be administered. Dr. Jones's suggestion of poison is asking us to believe Hackett somewhere, at some time during the day, drank poison given to him by someone he suspected to be responsible for Mr. Cardew's death. I'm not saying that theory is impossible, but it will take three or four days before you can have the analyst's report, and I'm sure you do not propose to let the case rest till then."

"No, that I do not," Strood declared. "Tomorrow I'll set about finding out all the places poor Hackett's been to this day."

"And tonight, sergeant – tonight we had better set about finding out just what that torn page in poor Hackett's notebook can tell us."

Strood was surprised.

"That, sir? That don't tell us much, not with so little left, does it? From what I saw out there the – the sense of it was in what's gone."

"Have you looked at it again?"

"No – ain't had time so far."

"Well, we *may* get the other half in the dyke tomorrow, but tonight we can see how much what's left can tell us. We owe that to Hackett, you know," he added, as the sergeant produced the notebook.

McNab laid the book on the table, right under the shaded lamp, and then stood back to look at it. The attitude was familiar to me. Often I had seen him stand away from some production or exhibit in just that fashion. So had I seen him act with a walking stick, a bit of broken glass, and, in the present case, so had he done yesterday with the blue velvet ribbon. Whether it was that he found stimulus to his imagination in regarding the thing from a distance, whether the distance left room for him to visualise the person or persons unknown who had, so to put it, gathered round the particular exhibit at the crucial moment, I cannot tell; but his practice with such concrete objects was invariable. He stood back as if to see the thing *all round*, as it were.

Strood had meanwhile held up his pipe to me in dumb petition. Signalling permission, I tiptoed over for the decanter. We had a drink together, the sergeant watching McNab with marked curiosity. The tired and drawn look went from Strood's face as he began to smoke, the facial muscles relaxing.

When McNab sat down he drew the notebook towards him and, turning over to a blank page, carefully tore it evenly from the book. This he put behind the half-page which he was studying, so that it gave him a view of just the amount of paper torn from the leaf on which Hackett had written. For one wild moment my thought was that he was about to write the missing words on this blank piece of paper. But, as presently appeared, this was a feat beyond even McNab's powers as yet. What he meant to do was merely to make evident to the eye the exact amount of space the lost writing would have occupied if we had had the entire page there before us.

Strood came round the table to stand behind McNab. Then only did he show consciousness of our presence at his back by a question to the sergeant:

"Of the ten lines, Strood, which would you like to see completed?"

Strood had ceased to pull at his pipe, and stood gazing down at the page in round-eyed wonder. He did not reply to McNab's query. I doubt if he heard it.

"Never thought it would give us as much information as that," he said. "Didn't notice it out there, I suppose."

"Well, it probably will tell us more than someone wants us to know," McNab said. "That is one penalty paid for removing the battery from Hackett's torch; he himself could not see very well when he got to work on the officer's book, and he was, I think, rather pressed for time. But which line would you like to see completed?"

Strood pointed with his pipe.

"There's one I don't need anybody to complete," he said, "and by good luck it's the most important – that one, the second."

"Oh, you think you know the missing words, then?"

"That's not hard, is it? Not like some of the crossword puzzles poor young Hackett used to solve, that ain't."

"So Hackett did crossword puzzles, did he?"

"He did, sir. Hackett was always keen to improve himself. It's not likely I'll ever have as promising a young officer again. And what's more, sir, I know this: if Hackett was here now he'd have had all the missing words added to that page already." Strood puffed thoughtfully for a moment, then nodded with conviction. "He was no fool, young Hackett wasn't."

The momentary quiver at the corner of McNab's mouth as he bent over the notebook showed me that he appreciated the sergeant's tribute to Hackett, even though it was expressed in terms not flattering to himself.

"Well, sergeant, what words would you put to the second line?" he meekly inquired.

Strood bent over and jabbed a huge thumb on the page.

"It only needs to have 'by' there, followed by 'Sn.' And that, with 'Mr. Card' added to the top line, tells us all we need to know," he said.

McNab wrote down the suggested additions on the blank page he had removed from the notebook and placed below the torn half. The lines then ran:

Mr. Cardew was murdered by Sneyd, as I thought. First the soft

Then he regarded the lines with great seriousness.

"I'm not sure I like it," he said, looking up.

"Why not, sir?" Strood demanded promptly. "That's what Hackett wrote, plain as a pikestaff."

"Well, 'by' is a word of only two letters, and, as you see, we've added only four letters to the second as against six in less space in the top, though Hackett had more to write in the second."

Strood narrowed his eyes on the book.

"But, sir," he cried, "you've only to put in a 'Mr.' in the second, as you've done in the first, to make it six all. Ain't that so?"

"That's so," McNab admitted. "But would Hackett have written 'Mr.' before Sneyd's name?"

"Why not? He was always polite, was young Hackett. Besides, it's regulations that even under arrest a prisoner is to be treated with respect."

It was clear to me that Strood's respect for McNab's perspicacity had received a shock.

"Very well, we'll pass those two first lines But 'Mr. Cardew was murdered by Mr. Sneyd' doesn't somehow sound probable to me. He may have written in the Christian name, of course, and made it Robert Sneyd."

Strood appreciated this suggestion. His fist thumped on the table.

"That's it, depend on it! It's what I'll say myself if it's given me to make the arrest. Robert Sneyd,' I'll say, 'it is my duty to—' You know the rest, I'll be bound. Certainly that's what he wrote there."

The other words were softly rubbed out and the new ones substituted; but I observed that McNab had to reduce their size to get them into the space available.

After a sip from his glass McNab passed on.

"It looks so simple that some of it frightens me, sergeant. Now take this third line. In its entirety it seems to read: *Campbell* gave me a clue'; but how does that connect with what precedes: *First* the *soft Campbell*'? Does that make sense? There are two Campbells, certainly; but is one of them known as – well, soft?"

Again Strood was thrilled.

"Ah, now you've hit it, sir – straight on the bull's eye, that is! I didn't myself see it at first. But your words bring back something to my mind."

Strood's broad face glowed with admiration.

"Well?" came impatiently from McNab.

"By that Hackett meant Mr. Percy Campbell beyond a doubt. It's like this, sir. When first he came to these parts some folks round about laughed when they heard what he'd come for: to set up a poultry farm for fancy fowls. And they *did*, at that time, call him soft for supposing he could make a living at it, not grasping the fact that his object was the breeding of valuable birds, and that he wasn't proposing to live off the sale of a few eggs, as it were."

It was at this point I saw how amply justified McNab was in taking the sergeant so minutely and slowly through the torn page in Hackett's book. But for this process that dim recess in Strood's brain might never have been stimulated into activity.

"And he still keeps on the poultry breeding?"

"Oh, yes, but the folks no longer call him soft for doing it. They know better now. Funny Hackett remembering that when I'd forgotten it."

Strood sighed gently. "But he was smart, poor Hackett was."

No comment came from McNab. He sat staring at the book before him so long that, but for his rigidity and the pucker about his narrowed eyes, I might have thought him asleep. Strood, after a time, glanced across at me, elevating his bushy eyebrows. I thought I knew what was in his mind.

"Is there any need to worry more?" I asked. "Surely, if Mr. Campbell gave Hackett a clue, he can give it to us as well."

McNab looked up like a person brought back from sleep.

"We can't depend on getting that," he said. "Mr. Campbell may not himself know he gave Hackett a clue. Look at that" –

his forefinger went to the second line – "Hackett uses the word 'First.' When was that? When did he pick up that first clue? Not today, I imagine."

"That's right, sir," Strood interjected. "Mr. Campbell hasn't seen Hackett today. I've ascertained that from Mr. Campbell himself."

"Very well; that certainly does not contradict what Hackett wrote down, for you may recognise that the two words, 'First' followed by 'then,' imply a process, a sequence. And, as I read it, what happened was this: *first* something Campbell let drop in a casual way later on started Hackett off on some scent, with the result that sometime today he lighted on something which *then* brought conviction. You see where we are? What Campbell gave him is of far less moment than the second thing, which clinched matters beyond all doubt. For in that second discovery there was real danger, as the words that follow show us; as, indeed, what happened to Hackett proves."

Strood's face fell.

"It don't seem so easy after all," he said.

Mechanically, McNab pulled out and began filling his pipe with his eyes still on the book.

"Oh, you can see Mr. Campbell tomorrow and try to get what he 'gave' in word, or action, or wink, or gesture, or nod, or hint, to Hackett. Why shouldn't you be able to pick up and follow the same clue?"

But the sergeant seemed dubious.

"He was a smart young fellow, was Hackett. Not fit to hold a candle for him, I'm not."

McNab liked to hear this generous tribute to the subordinate. He turned half round, laid a hand on Strood's arm, while with the other hand he held up the dead constable's notebook.

"Sergeant, isn't it Hackett who is here trying to hold the candle for you? And we're not going to waste the light he's given us – eh?"

The appeal went home to Strood like a shot from a gun.

"By George, you're right, sir!" he cried. "That's just what he tried to do – hold the candle for us. And I'm ready to go on with the digging till I drop."

So we went on with it!

"We may take it, then, as certain," McNab resumed, "that if only we knew what follows the word 'then' in the third line we would know how Mr. Cardew was murdered. Hackett is quite methodical even in the last entry he was ever to make in his book. First he sets down the name of the guilty man, and then he gives the method by which his crime was carried out. And the second particular is as essential as the first, for it must form the most weighty part of the evidence against him."

"That's right. Not much good knowing who did a thing unless you can prove how, and when, it was done."

"It's the 'how' that's the trouble. If only we knew the word to which that terminal 'g' belongs! Unfortunately, in the English language the words ending in 'g' are numberless. And, unfortunately too, as we descend the page we get less and less of what Hackett wrote, and the man who tore it out gets more and more. What does 'at the 8th' in the next line mean? We refer to a golf green in that way, but to nothing else I know of. The next line seems to bring in Cardew again, and in the following one the manager, Todd, appears to be mentioned in connection with the torch. After that so little of the page is left it is impossible to say whether the second warning is made in connection with the torch, or with the shoes. No, for all that I'll have to wait till morning – for a clearer head."

As he shut the book he looked up at me.

"Shoes again. Odd, isn't it?"

Strood picked up his cap and straightened himself.

"All I'll say, sir, is that I shouldn't like to be in that fellow's shoes with you after me. No, neither should I when I get my hands on him," he added truculently, swelling his chest.

McNab, I remember, stopped to look at him. Then, as the sergeant moved towards the door, he took his arm.

"Strood, my friend," he said quietly, "have you already forgotten what we said on the question of how it was done?"

The sergeant stopped, and both men faced each other just by the door.

"What do you mean, sir?"

He was obviously puzzled.

"Just this: I asked you to observe that though Hackett knew how it was done he, all the same, got caught himself. Didn't that fact tell you anything?"

The sergeant nodded slowly, very slowly, several times.

"I see what you mean. Yes, it does tell me something. It tells me there must be something damn clever in the way Mr. Cardew got done in – damn clever to trap young Hackett, and him knowing all the time what the trap was."

McNab looked satisfied.

"Right! So go warily. Remember the same danger is still there, alive and active. The man could have nothing in the world against Hackett, except that Hackett knew."

Chapter 15

It was a question by Detective Inspector Rawnsley which brought Rowland Todd under inspection. We had walked over to the New Romney police station for a conference, about ten the next morning; and for his information the whole case was restated, and the situation again passed under review. Finally, Inspector Rawnsley gave it as his opinion that the question of motive might open up a fresh, and more promising, line of investigation. This he said as he laid down the transcript of the shorthand report of the evidence taken at the inquest.

"There's this man Jippling, for instance," he remarked. "We must not overlook the fact that both tragedies occurred in close proximity to his house, and also that in both cases he, and he alone, made the discovery. Peculiar coincidence, isn't it?"

But this offended McNab's logic. Throughout the interview he had listened more than talked – much more; but this suggestion he could not pass.

"Well, inspector," he said, "I should say it would be still more peculiar if he had not been the discoverer, just because both tragedies happened so near his house."

And, as Rawnsley stroked his chin over this, Strood added deferentially:

"I think, sir, we can rule out Jippling. Anybody who knows Jippling knows he's incapable of it. He was a great favourite with the late Mr. Cardew too."

"Ah, and do you know if Mr. Cardew's favour extended so far as to appear in his will?"

We knew all about Mr. Cardew's bequests by this time. But the question was addressed to Strood.

"He left him two hundred pounds – for long and faithful service."

"There, you see. That at least gives us a sight at a motive. Motive is a very important factor, always, in such cases."

Strood looked at us apologetically, almost miserably.

"Oh, sir," he murmured, "if you knew George Jippling, you'd know! Besides," he added, "we have no reason to believe that Jippling knew Mr. Cardew had remembered him."

"Oh, very well. I only took the man at random, as an instance. It is, however, as well to remember that the smallness of the monetary gain is no criterion for ruling out the possibility of crime in any given case. Even a man of position may find himself in such urgent need of two hundred pounds as to be willing to proceed to extremities. To a person in this man Jippling's position it must seem a fortune." Then, as no one said anything, the inspector went on, "Oh, I don't suggest there was anything remiss, sergeant, but" – he coughed – "we'd better go through the names of the witnesses *seriatum*, on the question of motive alone." He turned over the transcript. "There's this Mr. Campbell, now. The son-in-law, I see."

"Stood to gain almost half the estate, sir, through his wife. We did apply the question of motive there," Strood proclaimed.

"To what extent?"

"Well, sir, to the extent of looking into the alibis of the two Mr. Campbells."

Here was something new. No wonder McNab sat up.

"With satisfactory results, of course?"

"The Yard did it for us, in London, and they were satisfied."

I myself avoided McNab's eye. If Strood had only known it, there was a man sitting beside him who, a Campbell being involved, had been far harder to satisfy than the Yard on this same alibi. But, for the inspector, the Yard sufficed.

"Good," he remarked, as he turned another page. "Ah, and about this Mr. Rowland Todd?"

"Nothing to gain by Mr. Cardew's death," Strood promptly replied.

"He was the deceased's manager, I see, and, I take it, stood to lose his job – his position, by the death?"

"Not exactly that, sir. As a matter of fact, Mr. Todd had resigned his position and Mr. Cardew had begged him to remain, offering an increase of salary. There had been some dispute between them. But the letter Mr. Cardew went out to post on the night of his death was a letter expressing his pleasure that Mr. Todd had withdrawn his resignation and accepted the offer of a higher salary."

"And the family are honouring this agreement, are they?"

"So I understand. Mr. Todd alone is capable of managing the business affairs."

"But no bequest was made to him?"

"None, sir."

"Then, on the question of motive, he is ruled out. Now, as to this young man, Sneyd, we do know how the question of motive applies to him. If you are right, sergeant, and I have carefully considered what you reported, he had the strongest motive of any; so far, that is, as we have discovered. He had a quarrel with Mr. Cardew, and of course he stood to gain about half the estate if he – well, pulled it off with the deceased's younger daughter. There we have two of the strongest motives, and many a man has met a violent death from either, alone."

The inspector pulled Hackett's notebook towards him and looked at McNab.

"I really do not see that we need go further than the second line of this," he asserted. "It is beyond reasonable doubt that the 'eyd' stands for Sneyd."

McNab agreed.

"That is not disputable," he said briefly.

Rawnsley seemed relieved by the reply. It was evident that Strood had fully posted up his D.D.I. with all that had passed between McNab and himself.

"Good," he said. "Good! Of course, I recognise that the question of getting at just what Mr. Campbell said, or did, to give Hackett the clue is a matter that may require delicate handling. On the other hand, Mr. Campbell may be able to tell us right away. In any case, I am myself going over to see Mr. Campbell presently; but I'd be glad to have you with me."

"Thank you," McNab said promptly. "I'll be equally glad to come – on one condition."

Rawnsley half frowned at the mention of conditions.

"Well?" he inquired with his eyebrows still slightly in the air.

"I come merely to listen."

Detective Inspector Rawnsley waved a hand.

"Oh, the sergeant has explained all that. I understand. Listeners see most of the game, eh?"

After that several details in the prosecution of the case were settled. Strood was instructed to set a man to keep observation on the house near the Littlestone golf links in which Sneyd lived. Rawnsley also suggested that by arrangement with Sneyd's landlady, or even without her knowledge, it might not be beyond the sergeant's power to obtain his fingerprints. He could not understand why this had not already been done in view of Sneyd's presumptive complicity. Strood was then instructed to inquire into Hackett's movements on the previous day, and have his report ready by the time the inspector returned from seeing Mr. Campbell.

Rawnsley was certainly a hustler. There and then he phoned through to Windygate and fixed up the interview with Mr. Campbell for two o'clock. Could not overhear the voice that replied to him, but I did observe that the inspector gave no explanation as to why he wished to come to Windygate.

"My hope is with Mr. Campbell," Rawnsley said after hanging up the receiver.

McNab nodded.

"Mine too," he said, "if he can suggest what may have given Hackett his clue."

About this Rawnsley, as we rose to leave, was optimistic.

"He has only got to retell all that passed between himself and the constable. Then, no doubt, between us, we can light on just the significant item – as Hackett himself did."

The inspector, in fact, was quite cheerful and, as I thought, not without reason. McNab, on the other hand, looked grave and rather perturbed. After some hesitation, he said:

"There's one point I'd like to see cleared up; it's about the manager, Rowland Todd." In some surprise we waited. "As between him and Sneyd, I mean," McNab went on. "Of the two, and on the question of motive, you decided that Todd did not stand to gain by Mr. Cardew's death."

"Well?" came from Rawnsley.

"But, as a matter of fact, he has gained. His position is more secure; for, as the sergeant told us, he is the only one now left who know's anything about all the buyings and sellings, and values of the stock."

Rawnsley pondered a moment, rubbing his chin.

"Yes," he said at last, "Todd is virtually master now, where he was servant before; but he could not know that in advance of Mr. Cardew's death."

"Quite," McNab agreed. "But was he less sure of it in advance than Sneyd was of – well, of pulling it off with Miss Ann Cardew?"

"We have no evidence of how sure Sneyd was of that."

"That is exactly the point," McNab said with great emphasis. "But there's another," he went on, "another thing I'm not easy about. You concluded that the evidence against Sneyd was unusually strong. I think myself it is; but, on the evidence so far before us, is it not also strong against Todd? Todd has, in fact, gained by the death; Sneyd, so far at least, has not done so. And, if Sneyd had a quarrel with Mr. Cardew, so, it appears, had Todd."

"A dispute," Rawnsley corrected.

"That is Todd's word for it, but a dispute that ends in resignation is, in effect, a quarrel."

"Not in this instance," Rawnsley nipped in; "Todd was reinstated."

"Yes, and like Pharaoh's baker, reinstated with increased emoluments and prestige. But that is going too quick. Do you know what the – dispute was about?"

Detective Inspector Rawnsley looked at Strood.

"Certainly, sir," Strood said. "Mr. Todd was quite frank about that. He told us Mr. Cardew questioned a certain payment – a matter of fifty odd pounds – which Mr. Cardew had forgotten. Mr. Todd said there had been several little differences between them, not connected with the accounts though, but he said that, in consideration of Mr. Cardew's ailing health, which made him irritable and suspicious, he himself had overlooked these petty differences. But when money was involved he thought he owed it to himself to resign. These were his very words. However, when Mr. Cardew discovered the error was his own, he made the most handsome apology."

McNab nodded.

"You saw Mr. Cardew's letter, then?"

"Well, no, sir. It had been destroyed. Naturally, as Mr. Todd said, when a dispute between two gentlemen is settled by an apology, one who is a gentleman does not preserve the written record of it for future use."

The inspector looked up from his writing, his mouth twitching at the rebuff thus given to McNab by the unconscious Strood.

"But," the sergeant concluded, "we have in this letter documentary evidence which fully supports Mr. Todd's statements."

He handed over a letter to McNab, who read it through with apparent care.

"May I have a copy?" he asked when he had finished.

Strood glanced at the inspector.

"Oh, yes; but, frankly, I don't see what all this is leading to," Rawnsley said.

McNab passed the letter for me to copy

HOTEL BRISTOL
READING

5th September

Dear Mr. Cardew,

I was sure you would discover your mistake sooner or later. That is why your words to me in the presence of Jippling did not wound, believe me, as much as you suppose. Of course I shall be willing to stay on at Redcotes, the interests of which must always lie nearest my heart. But there really was no need to offer me the two hundred pounds addition to my salary, though, of course, since you insist on it I am ready to give way in order to remain! Tomorrow I leave here for Brighton, but expect to be home in a day or two when we can talk this over.

Yours sincerely,

Rowland Todd

"Conclusive?" Rawnsley queried. "It was found among Mr. Cardew's letters."

"Seems so. It is dated the 5th; that is the Monday, two days before the death. Can I see the envelope?"

Strood, quite aware of why the envelope was wanted, passed it across. And I, taking the opportunity to give McNab the copy of the letter I had made, inspected the envelope over his shoulder. Yes, the envelope was in the same handwriting, on the same blue-grey paper, as the letter. It had been neatly slit open with a knife. More than that, it bore the Reading postmark; across the centre of the circle: 10 a.m. 5 Sept., and the word Reading ran half round the upper circumference. What McNab thought to make of it I could not guess, but it was beyond all doubt that the letter had been posted in Reading, and was in Mr. Cardew's hands the day before his death. This was so evident that I marvelled at the way McNab persisted in examining that envelope. To be sure he soon abandoned doubt, if he had any, of the postmark; but it seemed just perversity not to acknowledge at once that the police had been right not to waste time over Todd. His attempt to show that the case against Todd was as strong as the case against Sneyd was purely academic. And it seemed merely academic to me, even though I had a conviction from what I had seen of Todd at Redcotes, that Todd himself, no less than Sneyd, was strongly attracted by Miss Ann Cardew. However, after all his careful scrutiny of the envelope, he had to throw up his argumentation in the end.

"The date," he said, "is beyond dispute."

He looked rather crestfallen.

"Oh, you were quite right," Rawnsley said heartily as he rose. "It is far safer to question everything."

Strood showed us out. At the door he looked half reproachfully at McNab.

"If there had been anything in that Todd letter, sir," he said, "you might have trusted me to let you know about it."

"Of course I ought," McNab said. "Forgive me, sergeant; I should have known you would do all the routine business as it ought to be done."

We then struck out for Burrish. There was a wind behind us and the road made good walking.

"Sorry I hurt Strood's feelings," he said after a time.

"The inspector seemed satisfied with you," I said.

"Do you think so? Really, Chance? Now I should have said he half regrets having asked me to go to Windygate."

Privately, that is what I thought myself. For McNab had certainly not cut much of a figure at the conference. But I couldn't tell him so. Even a great man, as he used to say himself, has his smaller moments.

"Well," I said judicially, "I don't know about that. He gave you quite a pat on the back as we left."

He turned to stare at me.

"Did he? I didn't feel it."

"Verbally, I mean. When he said you were quite right to question everything."

"Oh, yes; that was a pat on the back. Wasn't it nice of him! The dear inspector, he meant it for an encouragement."

McNab's use of the word "nice" would, by itself, have been sufficient to tell me he spoke in humorous irony. For it was a word he never used in any serious connection.

But, if McNab could laugh at being patted on the back by Inspector Rawnsley, I could not. It rankled. And all the more because I thought that, for once, McNab had deserved that ignominy.

We were almost at the Woolpack when he suddenly pulled up with an exclamation of dismay.

"Now that's queer," he cried. "What made me forget that?"

"Forget what?" I demanded.

"Why, to make the suggestion that the inspector should arrange with the post office to have a first look at his letters before delivery."

"Whose letters? Todd's, do you mean?"

He shook his head reproachfully at me.

"No, no. Sneyd's, of course."

"Sneyd's!"

"Well, it's too far to walk back. We'll just go on to Redcotes and phone from there."

I followed, wondering, out of my depths.

And what happened when we reached Redcotes did not help me to recover my grip on the situation.

Chapter 16

McNab appeared to have forgotten all about telephoning his suggestion to the inspector as soon as we got to Redcotes. When Miss Ann Cardew entered the room into which we had been shown he talked with her for a little on a number of things, but not on any relevant to the case. The girl looked better. He got her to smile once or twice. Once, at a question of his which displayed a total ignorance of country life, she laughed outright. I liked her best when she laughed. They were sitting together on a divan, half facing each other. I wondered if Miss Cardew, as she sat with hands clasped over her knee, knew she was being closely studied. Pretty enough she was in that attitude, looking down, her head slightly to one side, at the neat little foot she unconsciously kept on the move.

"Miss Ann, I came to ask you a few questions."

The foot stopped swinging. I lost the fine contour of neck and chin her pose let me see.

"Yes?" she said, turning more towards him.

"You won't mind?"

"No," she replied frankly. "That official person, the—" She hesitated.

"The inspector, you mean?"

"Yes. He asked me so many, a few more won't hurt now. Probably I've answered most of yours already."

"I'll only put very necessary ones. Here is the first; Do you know whether Mr. Todd and Mr. Sneyd are on good terms with each other?"

Whatever questions she had previously answered, this could not have been one of them. The young woman was utterly taken aback. Her pale face flooded with colour. McNab's eyes were on her, not in an unkindly way.

"Well?" he said.

"No," she said, "I know they are not."

"Thank you, Miss Ann," he said; and to me it seemed that this was the reply he had hoped to hear. He went on, almost briskly: "Now, about the relations between Mr. Todd and your father—has there been any change latterly?"

She hesitated.

"If I said yes it would be unjust to Mr. Todd. It is quite true their relations did alter, for the worse; but Father was – well, very little put him out lately." She looked up. "I think I told you that."

"You mentioned George Jippling."

"That was one instance. I might have given Mr. Todd."

"Can you think why you didn't? Was it because Jippling's was the stronger example of the change in Mr. Cardew?"

"Yes."

"But Jippling wasn't dismissed. Mr. Todd was."

"Y—es."

"Well?"

"But Father was sorry afterwards about Mr. Todd, and wrote to ask him to come back."

"Did you hear him say he was sorry?"

"No. The letter was written when – when – I was in town seeing you."

"The second letter was. But an earlier one was sent to Mr. Todd at Reading."

"I knew nothing about either of them." She hesitated. "I must have mentioned Jippling because Father had real affection for him."

"Ah, I see now: that did make it a stronger example. How long would you say his irritation with Jippling lasted – a week or so?"

Her eyes widened.

"Oh, no. It never lasted like that, you know. Poor Father, he was always sorry about such things as soon as they were over."

McNab leaned forward.

"I want you to think before you answer this. You say, always. Can you remember a single exception?"

For quite a time Ann Cardew looked at the floor.

"No," she said at length. "No, I can remember none, except Mr. Todd."

McNab seemed pleased with the exception. It was certainly a most marked exception, since I knew myself from what I had heard Todd say at the inquest that the dispute could not have occurred less than five days before Mr. Cardew wrote his first letter to him – the one sent to the hotel at Reading. For at the inquest on the Saturday Todd stated that he had last seen Mr. Cardew about ten days previously, and his reply had been written on the Monday before Mr. Cardew's death. It was to this reply letter of Todd's that McNab now made his indirect approach.

"Miss Ann, you say you cannot remember a single instance except Mr. Todd. Do you mean the breach between him and your father was never healed?"

"No, no," she almost cried. "I only meant that it lasted longer; but it was healed."

"How do you know?"

There was real pain in her eyes, as well as surprise.

"Why, from the letter Mr. Todd wrote to Father," she said.

"He gave you the letter to read, then?"

"No. I read it only after the police inspector found it when going through the letters on Father's desk."

"You knew about the disagreement between him and Mr. Todd?"

"Yes. He couldn't hide a thing like that. He had to mention it. He was like that."

"Quite." McNab nodded with slow thoughtfulness. I knew something had come to him. But to guess what it could be was beyond me.

"Could you show me just where the letter was found?" he asked next. "Was it in his study?"

She stared blankly at him.

"Certainly; in his study with the other letters," she said. And when he waited she got on her feet. "You can see for yourself. They told us not to touch the room yet," she added, leading the way across the hall into a corridor opposite.

The study must have been one of the smallest rooms in the house. One large bookcase occupied the side facing the window, but the walls were mostly covered with framed photographs of cricketing groups. By the side of the fireplace hung a bat with a silver inscribed plate on it, while a bureau desk stood on the right, between window and fireplace. Neatly stacked on the flat of the desk were some half-dozen piles of letters.

McNab exclaimed when he saw them: "How very neat!"

Mistaken I may have been, but it seemed to me there was a touch of disappointment in his tone. Miss Ann gave a little sigh.

"Poor Father," she breathed. "No, he didn't keep things orderly like that – not latterly at least. The officer arranged them so, each day's letters by themselves."

McNab bent down to look at them.

"Yes," he said, "I see. Monday, Tuesday and Wednesday in the back row, and those he himself handled, those which came on Thursday and Friday, in front." He stared hard, for a full minute. "Now, can you say from which set Mr. Todd's letter was taken?" he asked, turning to her.

"From this one," she replied, putting a finger on the Tuesday's letters.

"Did your father always open his own letters?"

"Always. But of course those in front were not opened by him." She indicated the Thursday and Friday piles.

McNab nodded sympathetically.

"So I see," he murmured, in a way that made me prick up my ears.

He took up the Tuesday lot and counted them.

"Eleven – twelve with Mr. Todd's letter," he remarked.

Then, omitting the Wednesday pile, he ran over Thursday's.

"Nine." He laid them down softly, then turned with decision after staring vacantly for a minute or two. "That's all, I think," he said, glancing at his watch.

"Won't you both stay and have some lunch? Mr. Campbell and my sister are coming over."

McNab was decided.

"Thank you, no; I must catch the 1.20 post at our collecting box. But I would have liked to talk one or two things over with Dr. Campbell," he added regretfully.

"Oh, he's not coming; he has gone to town."

McNab almost dragged me away. Ann Cardew saw us out, and stood in the doorway looking after us. She made a pretty picture standing there, her hands behind her back, and with wonder in her eyes.

But I had something to wonder about myself, though it could not spring from the same cause as Ann Cardew's. We had not gone far from the house before I put it to him.

"I thought it was Sneyd's correspondence you were concerned about," I said; "not Todd's or Mr. Cardew's."

"Why?"

"You came here to phone a suggestion about it."

"Well, I changed my mind, you see"

"Why?" I was pleased with that echo of his own question.

"Because of what we both heard and saw, first at the police station and then, just now, in Mr. Cardew's study." He held up a silencing hand.

"You heard what I heard, saw what I saw. If you made nothing of it you'll have to wait. I'm reserving my breath for that postman."

We plodded on for another five minutes, I wondering if Ann Cardew had been more understanding than myself. Before we reached Burrish I had concluded she had been, not because her intelligence was superior, but simply because she had an inside knowledge of the case which, so far, I was without.

When we reached the bridge at Burrish I saw the postman standing at his cottage door. He was lighting his pipe in the manner of a man who has just finished a hearty meal. His bicycle stood against the wall, and he was evidently waiting for the time at which he was due to make the 1.15 collection from the bridge pillar box before returning to the New Romney office.

"Good day, postie," McNab saluted him affably.

"Day, sir," the man returned.

"Just been having an argument with my friend here over a post office regulation," he said. "Perhaps you can settle it."

"Perhaps I might," the man returned cautiously.

"Well, look at this letter." Here he produced a letter from his inside pocket. "It was delivered to me in London as you see it. What would you do down here if you got a letter in that condition to deliver?"

The postie took the letter in his hand, evidently puzzled, turned it over, examined back and front, then looked up.

"You don't go for to tell me they delivered it open," he said.

"Just as you see it."

"Well, there now! It couldn't have been noticed surely, or they'd have marked it *Found open*."

McNab turned to me.

"Isn't that what I said?" he demanded triumphantly.

"Well, I admit I was wrong," I said, taking the cue.

Postie smiled deprecatingly.

"Of course they're mighty busy up in London; easy for them in the rush and hurry of having hundreds to handle. They can hardly take an interest in each letter, same as we do down here, where we're not nigh so busy," he explained,

"London being a very busy place."

The esprit de corps which formed the basis of this elaborate defence of his town confreres amused me.

"They say you read all the postcards," I said laughingly.

"What me, mister? I deny it. I ain't no Peeping Tom, and if there's anybody has—"

McNab hastened to soothe the rising wrath.

"No, no; nobody says that of you. Besides, we're not talking of post cards, but of envelopes. Now, about that letter you delivered last Tuesday."

"What letter?" Postie demanded suspiciously.

"It was in a blue-grey envelope, an uncommon colour."

"Don't know nothing about it." He was almost surly now.

"Well, now, look here. My friend wasn't suggesting that you, personally, read post cards; what he meant was merely that, for an intelligent man like you, there's something between taking too little interest in the letters you deliver and taking too much."

"The happy medium." Postie nodded, mollified.

"That's it. Now, take this letter of mine. You say, if it had passed into your hands cut open along the top, you'd have it marked *Found open*."

"If I saw it."

"Quite. But if the flap had been accidentally left unstuck by the sender?"

Postie grinned diffidently.

"Well, sir, I dare say I'd just give it a lick myself. You know what people are. Least said soonest mended's a good motto."

McNab nodded.

"I agree. Now, you remember last Thursday, I suppose?"

The man, suddenly grave, said:

"It would be queer if I didn't. 'Twas the day after Mr. Cardew died."

"And you will remember well the letters you delivered that day at Redcotes?"

"I might," he replied, a certain uneasiness appearing on his face.

McNab shot the next question at him.

"Do you remember one in a blue-grey envelope from Reading, with *Bristol Hotel, Reading*, printed on the flap?"

"There was no letter like that, sir."

His bearing had become sullen, almost hangdog, quite abruptly.

"Ah, you've forgotten, have you!"

McNab's face frowned in disappointment. The postman looked at his watch and moved towards his bicycle, hitching his bag over his shoulder. He was evidently hurt at McNab's suggestion that he could forget. It was but a few yards over the bridge to the pillar box, and we walked behind till we reached it. McNab watched him as he stooped to open it and extract the contents. The man was a long time over the job. Then he rose and faced us as we stood behind him.

"You'll excuse me, gentlemen," he said quietly. "You got me to talk before I knew what you was after. Not till you mentioned Redcotes, I didn't. But I've told you the truth. Whether you're police or post office inspectors is all the same; I swear to it, I delivered all the letters given me last Thursday."

"And how many were there?" McNab demanded.

"Ten," he declared. "If any letter is missing, I didn't take it; and," he added, again hesitating, "as for Mr. Todd, he's surely a gentleman beyond suspicion."

This unexpected mention of Todd I set down as one of the big surprises of this case. To me it was so. And I fancy it was a surprise to McNab himself, though he may have revealed less of what he felt.

"So you handed over the Thursday letters to Mr. Todd?" he said.

"No, sir," came eagerly. "That's against regulations. What happened was just a little accident at the Woolpack. I had one letter for Mrs. Beddoes, and I was just taking it from the bundle in my left hand as I stepped inside the door when Mr. Todd happened to be coming out, in a hurry, saying something to young Ben over his shoulder. He walked clean into me, sending the letters flying, and me too."

"Dear me, how clumsy of him! But I suppose he picked up the letters for you?"

"He did, sir, and was very sorry; begged my pardon too."

"And they were the Redcotes letters which fell?"

"That is so, Redcotes being the next house to the Woolpack, for all the distance between."

Postie's eyes were anxiously fixed on McNab's face. It certainly was stern now.

"Well," he said after a moment's consideration, "we accept your explanation. It may be that the letter was never sent from Reading. Indeed, I am now quite certain that is the explanation. So" – he nodded, with an encouraging official wave of the hand – "you can regard the matter as settled. You will hear no more about it – from us."

For a minute I watched the happy postman pedalling hard along the New Romney road.

McNab stood, as if rooted to the spot, in a sort of daydream.

"Do you consider that was quite legitimate?" I demanded when I got tired of waiting.

"Legitimate – what?" he asked, beginning to move.

"Frightening that poor fellow into believing we were high postal officials."

"It was his own assumption, that. Besides, he has gone away happier than he was before I spoke to him."

And it is not to be denied that in this McNab was right. We made towards the Woolpack, seeing Mrs. Beddoes standing in the door looking about for us. We were very late for lunch.

"It was certainly Todd who took that letter," I said, "and just in this very doorway. That stumble against the postman was a fake, and had been all thought out in advance."

He stared at me, a queer amused look glinting in his eyes.

"Don't you think so?" I asked, surprised at his silence.

"I'm thinking quite a lot of things. One of them is that even clever men have their foolish moments."

That was so like him – to leave it uncertain to whom he referred, himself or Todd.

Chapter 17

Knowing well the mood in which McNab was, I did not at lunch make any attempt to force the conversation. And the meal was not of the leisurely sort, since we were late and had to get to Windygate for the interview with Mr. Campbell. Yet McNab, short as the opportunity was, did not neglect a moment. He had made for himself a rough copy of the page from Hackett's notebook, and this he kept propped up before his eyes against the water-jug while he ate. He is, I said to myself, reviewing it in the light of what he has discovered this morning. But as to whether that light was derived from Miss Ann or the postman, or both, I could not tell. What I was sure of, however, was that Rowland Todd had become deeply involved; and I watched to see what particular line of Hackett's book engaged McNab's eyes.

It was, I found, impossible to tell on so small a surface as that page presented what line riveted those eyes. Yet I did see, at least, that his whole attention was given, not, as before, to the upper half, but to the bottom of the page. He appeared to be trying to force continuity of sense into the broken words left by the dead policeman. Once his fork, stopping halfway on its journey, appeared to be forgotten and remained in mid-air, in the most grotesque way, while he stared at the page.

"*Todd, my torch*," he quoted. "It is only in the dark, anyway, that a torch is used. *Take care*. How? Is it advice to *use shoes*? Where? And *at 150 feet*. Now, why that length?"

Suddenly the fork fell into his plate with a rattle that made me jump.

"My God," he whispered, "a hundred and fifty feet. Oh, Hackett, we don't measure it by feet, but by yards. Yes, you should have said fifty yards, then I'd have guessed what that word line meant. Yes, and what the word before it was, though only the final 'g' is left. '*Washing* line' is what I guessed! Not much!"

But I couldn't sit still any longer.

"Do you understand it all now? For God's sake, Mac, do tell me. No details – just say yes or no."

"Oh," he said dispassionately, "I think I've got something – quite a small thing as yet – out of it. Enough to try an experiment tonight, if you are game?"

"Anything, anything," I asserted.

"It will be – dangerous. Hackett warned us – twice. And he didn't do it too often, Godfrey; not too often, if what I make out of it is right. But don't ask me about it yet, not till after – after I've seen Rawnsley."

He rose, as if the mention of Rawnsley had reminded him of our appointment at Windygate.

"I don't need to ask who the man is, anyway," I said pointedly.

"That's good – quite clever, that," he said. "But with me it's more concern now to know and prove *how* he worked the thing. As yet I have only a glimmer, Chance, just a wee bit glimmer of light, as yet."

I took this for his usual cautious understatement. In any case, I felt confident. For what I argued was that, with this glimmer already in his possession, he was more likely to pick up the clue which Hackett had got from Mr. Campbell.

And it was in this belief that I hurried him out of the inn and up the road to Windygate. To me at least the sharp walk did good. My nerves needed the steadiness that comes from the rhythmic monotony of a quick, steady walk. By the time we reached the house I was no longer jumpy with anticipation of speedy developments.

The Campbells had got back from Redcotes, but it was Mrs. Campbell who received us in the sunny drawing room into which we were shown. She was not sitting there alone, though, at first, curious as I had grown about Ann Cardew's sister, I did not observe the man. Mrs. Campbell physically resembled her sister in everything, perhaps, except size. She was cast in a larger mould; yet a mould, as it were, of the same pattern. Slower in her movements, slower in her speech too, there was about her that indefinable air of lethargic dignity which often earns for the big, handsome woman the epithet "queenly."

"My husband is out somewhere. You know Mr. Sneyd?" she said, with a movement of her hand.

Mr. Sneyd bowed a trifle stiffly, if not defiantly. But McNab, obviously to Sneyd's surprise, put out his hand. After that the usual banalities about the weather flowed smoothly for a time.

Sneyd gravitated into talk with McNab, who, unlike myself, had no unpleasant associations for him. Mrs. Campbell watched them, I noticed, while they stood in the bay window looking out on the trim, sunlit lawn. A pause came in our own talk, and she turned to me.

"I know Mr. Campbell asked you over to see the place," she said. "But you won't see it at its best just now."

"Of course," I said. "He – must be so busy."

"Oh, yes, there's so much on his hands – business matters that keep him constantly coming and going. You are interested in poultry?"

A glance showed me she wasn't laughing at me: her face was quite serious.

"Well," I rejoined, "I don't know much about poultry, beyond the eggs."

"Ah, but the incubators are interesting. Mr. Campbell is very proud of his hobby, and delights to explain every detail. There are times when he thinks of nothing else."

For all the smiling mouth I detected a note of bitterness, if not mockery, in her voice.

Sneyd turned round.

"Shall I go and get Percy, Mrs. Campbell?" he asked.

She hesitated in replying. I saw McNab look up. The question seemed to have surprised Mrs. Campbell, for I distinctly heard at my side a sharply indrawn breath. It was an odd moment, somehow.

"Y – es," she said at last, "perhaps you'd better, Mr. Sneyd."

Then indeed I recognised what was taking place. They were talking over our heads, these two. More things were being said between them than the mere words used conveyed. There was an underlying significance in the formality with which each used the other's surname. And as I looked at the woman, while for the briefest moment they held each other's eyes, it was easy to see the challenge in hers.

Sneyd nodded.

"Very well," he said; "I dare say he's not far off."

"May I come too?" McNab begged. "The garden is so pretty."

They stepped through the French window at the side of the bay on to the lawn, and the moment of queer by-play was over. Wheels within wheels, I was saying to myself when she looked round at me, once more smiling.

"Mr. Campbell is so vain about his incubators – like a child with a new toy, I often tell him."

She had an irresistible smile.

"But," I said, "unlike the child, he hasn't tired of his toy."

She shook her head with a sigh.

"It absorbs him so; he rushed out the moment we got back."

Then, as we began to rattle out small talk about Burrish and its ways, and characters like Zacchary Moss, it struck me she knew about Rawnsley's telephone message – and was afraid on Sneyd's account. The thought followed that the detective inspector and McNab might not find it so easy to pick up Hackett's clue from Campbell. Both had said their hope was in Campbell. But Campbell could not now be unaware of the suspicion the police held in regard to Sneyd, and it was highly improbable, I thought, that he would rack his brains to remember what would incriminate Sneyd.

On the whole, I considered that we had a better chance of striking the clue if Campbell did not know what the clue was, and McNab, as I knew, was fairly shrewd in getting down below a surface plausibility. But then I remembered Campbell's evidence at the inquest – how deftly he turned the tables on the coroner – and I doubted.

A motor-horn sounded out on the road just as the door opened, and Campbell came forward to me with outstretched hand.

"Glad to see you, Mr. Chance," he said, giving me a friendly grip.

McNab, it appeared, had walked down to meet Rawnsley. Nothing was said of Sneyd.

"Mrs. Campbell has been telling me about your hobby," I said.

"Did she call it that?" he asked, looking reproachfully at her. "It's something more than that, you know. Ah, well," he went on, "perhaps there will be time to show you what a serious scientific business it can be after we've finished with this fellow Rawnsley."

On that he carried me off to the room set apart for the interview.

The smoking room had very comfortable-looking divan chairs. But it was perhaps symptomatic of the intensity of our feelings that we did not sit in those inviting chairs; none of us, that is, except McNab. Campbell took one end of a high oak settle backing the window, at the other end of which I had planted myself. As for the inspector, he was soon on his feet in the middle of the hearth rug, and with no beating about the bush he came to the purpose of his visit.

"We need your help, Mr. Campbell," he said; "help that you alone can give, I believe."

Campbell nodded alertly, bowing to me.

"Mr. Chance, here, who was, I think, first on this case, already knows how anxious I am to help," he said.

Rawnsley then, with his hands behind his back, went on at once to outline the entire situation. I must say that the masterly ease and certainty with which he marshalled the various facts won my admiration. It had the stamp of the best professional manner, even to the dry, level, unemotional voice, which detailed every known fact and played lightly round such inferences as might be drawn from them. And then, when the rapid yet admirably lucid resume had ended, Rawnsley produced Hackett's notebook, turned up the all-important page, and laid the book on Campbell's knees.

"And now, sir," he said, "the rest lies in your hands."

At first Campbell gave us no sign as to whether he did or did not recall what he had said that supplied Hackett with his clue. Probably his imagination had been too strongly touched by Rawnsley's story of the officer's death, and certainly it did strike at one's emotions to look on that torn page, with the dead officer's attempt at a message. I knew what I myself would have felt had I seen my own name there recorded as one who had helped him in his work. And Campbell was looking at other names as well – those of Rowland Todd and Robert Sneyd, though they assuredly were not mentioned on that page in the same honourable way.

That was a tense moment. Both Rawnsley and McNab had their eyes on him. As he bent over the page the upstanding Rawnsley could, of course, see no more than the top of his thick auburn hair, though McNab, in the low, luxurious divan, may have seen a little more. I myself, sitting on his right, and at his own level, saw only the strong chin and the stiff, straight line of his mouth. But he was obviously anxious to assist us, for he seemed to be thinking hard.

Set down in words, as I have had to do, that moment of desperate tension must seem long. And no doubt it seemed intolerably long to both Rawnsley and McNab. To Rawnsley as to whether Mr. Campbell's witness would clinch the case against Sneyd; to McNab, who did not believe in Sneyd's guilt, as to whether it would confirm his suspicions against Todd or some person as yet unsuspected.

At last he looked up.

"I'm trying to think – to disentangle things," he said.

"No hurry," Rawnsley nodded encouragingly.

"You see," he went on, "I've seen quite a lot of Hackett lately. He's been friendly with our parlourmaid, a nice girl, who's so grieved and shocked by what has happened that my wife has sent her home for a day or two. Well, it's not easy to recall even the occasions on which I've talked to poor Hackett, much less all we talked about – not off-hand, like this, at least."

"Better begin with the last occasion," Rawnsley suggested.

Mr. Campbell nodded.

"Exactly what I've been doing. It was on Sunday night, about 8.30. We had been out and were having a scratch supper. You know the sort of thing probably – more or less waiting on ourselves. But we wanted something from the kitchen, and I rang. What *was* the thing, now?" Campbell frowned in the effort to remember. "Yes, I've got it. Alice – that's the maid, you know – had taken off a plate Sneyd wanted."

"Mr. Sneyd was there?" Rawnsley interjected.

"Oh, yes; he'd come round. Well, Alice had carried away a plate he was using for his biscuit and cheese, and I rang for it – twice. Then I went myself for it, and found Hackett in the kitchen. Hackett seemed to be helping her with the plates, and they hadn't heard the bell." He smiled a sad little smile. "Rather amusing at the time, it was, to see them with their heads together; Hackett was so abashed, poor chap. So I sent Alice in with the plate, and stayed a moment or two with him to put him at his ease."

"Was it the same plate?" Rawnsley inquired.

The question, of course, surprised Campbell.

"That I couldn't tell you," he said.

Rawnsley waved a hand.

"We'll pass that now. Possibly Mrs. Campbell can tell us if a plate is missing. Now, what exactly passed between yourself and Hackett in the few moments you were with him?"

Mr. Campbell looked down at the notebook on his knees, round which his arms were clasped. I think we all knew what was happening to him. It was a moment I, in a lesser degree, well enough knew: the moment when we are called on to search the mind for something of first-rate importance, and we hesitate, afraid, as it were, to lift the lid and see if the wanted thing is there at all.

Finally Campbell shook his head.

"I don't like this," he said, in apparent distress; "I don't like it at all."

"We must, I'm afraid, press for all you can tell," Rawnsley said firmly.

"No doubt, oh, no doubt! But do you realise what it means to me to have to say something that may send a man to the gallows, a man who may have been on friendly terms with me?"

"We are searching for the man who killed Mr. Cardew," Rawnsley said with quiet significance.

Mr. Campbell accepted that fact.

"True, quite true, inspector; but that doesn't help me, you know. If what I said could bring Mr. Cardew back to life again," he cried, nervously clasping and unclasping the fingers round his knees, "or even if I—" He pulled up.

"Will you finish, please, Mr. Campbell. You were saying 'even if I.' "

"Well, what I meant to say that that – well, I see that what I may say here and now won't, perhaps, end here and now. What

I mean is that what I say now, in private, may have to be repeated in a criminal court. If you could give me an assurance that I will not be put into the witness box, it would be easier."

Rawnsley nodded in sympathy.

"I see what you mean," he said. "Very unpleasant position for a former friend to be in. But I'm afraid, Mr. Campbell," he added, "the only assurance I can give is that, if we see any way to avoid it, we'll not put you in the witness box."

Then McNab joined in.

"There is a way, inspector," he said. "You can safely give Mr. Campbell the assurance he asks for."

Rawnsley, obviously relieved, but at first showing more surprise than relief, stared hard at McNab. So did Mr. Campbell.

"You see a way?" he asked quickly,

"I do."

"Very well," Mr. Campbell said slowly, "that makes it easier for me."

But Inspector Rawnsley would have no misunderstanding.

"*I'm* not giving you such an assurance, because I cannot give it; but this I'll say, Mr. Campbell: if this gentleman," indicating McNab, "sees a way out, you can take it as certain such a way exists and is practicable I can give you my word on that, anyhow."

This was handsomely said on Rawnsley's part; yet, for all the tone of certainty in the inspector's utterance, Campbell examined McNab, studied him, in fact, for quite a while, as if to be certain for himself.

"Well," he said ultimately, "I must be content with that hope. You will appreciate my position, gentlemen. I am speaking in the dark, as it were, quite unaware of how the constable got his clue from me, but very well aware that I may be called on to give evidence that may put a rope round a former friend's neck. And I confess that, no matter how much he may deserve it, personally I'd rather be out of it." He looked at us all in turn, almost wistfully; but, though I imagine he read sympathy in each of us, he also found us waiting for him to go on. His eyes went back to Hackett's book.

"Ah, well, the question was: what passed between Hackett and myself in the kitchen."

"As exactly and as fully as you can remember," Rawnsley begged.

Campbell considered.

"The first thing I remember was making a small joking remark to Hackett. Seeing him holding the plate, I asked if he had come as substitute for the cook, or something like that, the cook having her evening off on Sundays. Then I said to Alice that a man so ready to help with the plates would make a first-rate husband. That sent her scurrying to the dining-room. To put Hackett at his ease – for he had blushed as much as the girl – I asked him if he knew what made the coroner adjourn the inquest on the previous day. His reply was that it was to allow time for further investigations, which of course I already knew. Then—"

"One moment," Rawnsley interrupted. "Am I right in taking it that you were alone with the officer all through?"

"Yes. It was the cook's night off, so we were alone till Todd came in."

McNab looked up sharply at Mr. Campbell, whose eyes were now on the book lying on his knees.

"Go on, please," came from the eager inspector.

"Of course, when Hackett asked a question about the eighth green on the Littlestone golf links, I took it merely as an attempt to head me off from prying into the police investigations. The question he asked was why I so often began my round from the eighth green. My reply was that I only did so when playing with Mr. Sneyd, who lives at Mrs. Upcott's house, which is practically alongside that green. Beginning our round from the tee there, we ended on the eighth, and then usually dropped into the house for refreshments. But when Hackett said the police were about to take *a strong line* in regard to a certain person, I saw he attached importance to the eighth green."

"Did he mention the name of the person?"

"Oh, no; no name was mentioned."

"But could you guess?"

A look of distress appeared on Mr. Campbell's face.

"I had hoped," he said, "that you would confine your questions to matters of fact, and not to my guesses."

"Quite right, Mr. Campbell; please continue."

Campbell nodded acceptance of the apology.

"Well, about the taking a strong line, I said it would be well to *take care*. This he misunderstood. He said he knew there was death waiting for the unwary who got mixed up in the affair, evidently referring to the strange manner of Mr. Cardew's death; but what I meant was that hasty action might discredit the police. Just as I was about to explain this a knock came, and Mr. Todd entered. Something had gone wrong with the ignition of his motorcycle, and he had come, he said, to borrow a lamp. Not another word after that was said about the case. Hackett volunteered to lend Todd his torch. They both then left the house, and I returned to the dining room."

"That was the last you saw of him?"

"Yes."

Inspector Rawnsley's fine brow furrowed in thought.

"It all fits in," he said; "harmonises, I mean, with the entry in Hackett's notebook. And it stops just where he went off with Mr. Todd; but so far I do not see how you gave him a clue at all, Mr. Campbell."

"I don't see it myself," said Campbell. "But is it certain he meant that *I* gave it him? You assume, I take it, that the three letters, the 'ell' on this page, are the last letters in my name. But there are many words ending in 'ell' – bell and dwell and farewell and – well, knell and *hell*, if you like!"

To judge by Rawnsley's face this last word was the very one he himself might have suggested. But of course Campbell was simply making a heroic, but very lame, effort to head them off from Sneyd. Anyone could see that; and for a time nothing was said; it might have been thought, indeed, that we were all searching in our minds for more likely words ending in "ell" than the ones Mr. Campbell had suggested. McNab at all events seemed to have been so engaged.

"And *shell*," he suggested, with quite portentous gravity.

I very nearly laughed. Rawnsley, even in his moment of disappointment, smiled. No wonder he did, if McNab, after the long interval, could only suggest one word, and that one a word as unlikely as any of those cited on the spur of the moment by Mr. Campbell himself!

McNab's contribution was, at all events, an anticlimax that brought the interview to an end. Rawnsley picked up from the floor the notebook, which had fallen from Mr. Campbell's knees when he heard McNab's absurd suggestion. Campbell, unlike Rawnsley, did not smile at it, but I am sure from the way his mouth twitched that he wanted to laugh as much as I did myself.

"We must think over what you have told us," Rawnsley said. "Possibly I may have to see you again later."

Mr. Campbell, with the inspector, led the way from the room, McNab and myself in the rear. Then abruptly a change came over the situation. We saw, along the passage, our host and the inspector join Mrs. Campbell, who was talking to Todd in the hall. The sight pulled McNab up, and, drawing me back, he fished out his little packet of cigarette papers.

"See that Todd comes with you," he whispered in sudden eagerness, "when Mr. Campbell shows you round his place."

Before I could say a word he was stepping quickly to the door. He had a leaf from his cigarette papers between his fingers, and was rapidly tearing it into small pieces as he went out.

Chapter 18

That moment when McNab slipped out by the side door was, I now know, the decisive moment in the whole case. But, at the time, what I saw was only that McNab must have extracted something new out of the interview. That bewildered me. I could not guess what it could be, for I saw all Mr. Campbell had said had left Inspector Rawnsley a most disappointed man.

Yet before following the others into the drawing room I had time to recognise two things quite clearly: Mr. Campbell's frank and full account of what had taken place between himself and Hackett might have given McNab the same clue as Hackett himself picked up. That was the first thing I saw, and saw with a thrill of exaltation. The second thing was that McNab's suspicion centred round Todd, whereas Rawnsley's mind was preoccupied with the conviction of Sneyd's guilt. And the case against Sneyd was so strong that its very strength might have blinded the inspector to the significance of any new fact which pointed away from Sneyd to someone else.

I had, however, no time to speculate as to what McNab had got hold of, though I entered the room wondering what on earth he was going to do with his cigarette paper.

"Ah, there you are," Mr. Campbell greeted me. "We're to have some tea before the inspector goes."

Mrs. Campbell looked up.

"But it's not quite ready," she said. "You've just time to show them round," she added to her husband.

Mr. Campbell appeared to have forgotten he had invited me to Windygate for that very purpose.

"Well," he said, "there's not much to see at this time of the year." He looked at me doubtfully. "Still, if you think—"

"I'd like a look round very much," I said heartily.

Todd here acknowledged my presence with an off-hand nod.

"Thought your friend was here too," he remarked.

"He is, but I think he's gone out to smoke a cigarette," I said.

"Oh, he needn't have done that," Mrs. Campbell said with hospitable protest as she touched the bell.

Todd smiled.

"But, having done it, we may as well follow his lead," he said, offering his cigarette case to Rawnsley. "Let's go and find him."

There was something odd about that moment. There was, somehow, strain and tension in it. What it was I could not tell; but the sight of that cigarette case brought back sharply the remembrance of the unclaimed cigarette case found on the Redcotes road, and this, when I recalled McNab's behaviour with his own cigarette papers, left me curiously disquieted and mystified.

Yet, once we were outside and found McNab pacing up and down smoking in quiet meditation, it all seemed normal enough. Todd, on being introduced, smiled quite affably.

"You like the fresh air," he said.

McNab agreed with a nod.

"I do," he said. "Even in the country I sleep with my windows as wide as they'll go."

"And his bed half out of the window too," I said, gathering from the seriousness with which McNab spoke that he wished them to believe this was his sole motive for going out after the long and stuffy interview.

But all the time, as Mr. Campbell led us round, exhibiting the various appliances he used for his scientific poultry breeding, I was wondering what McNab had been up to. That he had been setting a trap for Todd I had guessed; and it was on Todd I kept my eyes – on him, that is, while not actually casting about to see what McNab had done with the torn pieces of his cigarette paper.

We did come on them at last. Outside a long wooden house Mr. Campbell paused, with his hand on the door.

"Hardly worthwhile going in here," he said "At this season there's nothing going on."

"What is it?" McNab asked.

"The incubation house."

"Oh," I said, "Mrs. Campbell advised me to see that."

With a consenting nod, he pushed open the door.

"Really, you know," he remarked as we entered, "Todd here, or even Sneyd, is more up in the latest developments in this sort of work than I am now. At least, so my doctor-brother says."

McNab laughed.

"That means you got bored with it, I suppose," he said. "Well, perhaps, if I had my own hobby so close to my door, that might be my fate too."

Mr. Campbell smiled in his turn.

"And what is yours?"

"Angling," McNab replied, with a sigh.

"Ah! I would not tire of that – if only I had water near enough."

"Good Lord," Todd cut in, "hear the man say that – with the sea almost lapping his own doorstep!"

A look of mutual understanding, followed by a smile, passed between McNab and Campbell. But nothing more was said about fishing, to my relief; for I was all on edge to get on with our inspection. And, as it proved, I was correct in my guess: the torn cigarette papers were there.

At first I didn't see them, not till my eyes got used to the subdued light of the interior. But I had not been more than a couple of minutes listening to Mr. Campbell's very lucid explanations before I saw Todd's cigarette on the floor. Whether he had thrown it down, or whether it had fallen, I could not say, but it lay on the ground, close up to one of the tiered glass-sided boxes, and beside it I saw, littered about, what looked like fragments of the rice paper I had seen McNab tear up in the passage.

After that I lost the thread of Mr. Campbell's explanation. His even voice kept on, and to me was no more than a meaningless drone, for all my attention concentrated itself on Todd. And, after all, all that happened was that Todd put his foot on the fallen cigarette. Then, nonchalantly, with his hands in his pockets, he began to supplement something Mr. Campbell was saying to Rawnsley and McNab, who seemed about equally bored. Nothing happened.

When, half an hour later, we left the house together, it was in reference to the failure of his experiment with the paper that I said, in imitation of a grocer serving a customer:

"And the next?"

There was, I suppose, something offensive in the jaunty, ironical tone of my question. I could not help it. The truth was my pride had been wounded – not my personal pride, but my pride in him; for he had cut an unheroic figure that day, not only in the earlier New Romney conference on the case, but also in the interview with Mr. Campbell. And it seemed clear from the complete failure of his experiment that the inferences which had led him to make it must have been fallacious. Yet he replied to my satiric question in exactly the equable tone a customer might have replied to the grocer:

"Half a pound of keel, please."

This took the wind out of my sails.

"What on earth do you mean?" I asked, not in the least like a grocer.

"Och," he said, "that's what we call it in Scotland, but I believe every county in England has a different name for it. In Dorset, for example, they call it reddle."

"But what in Hades is it?"

"Keel? Oh, it's just the variously coloured stuff they use for marking sheep. It's the red kind I'm after."

This was altogether too much for me. Vaguely, my bewildered mind went back to my first meeting with Sergeant Strood, and the talk we had about sheep stealing. But, though I could make nothing of it all, it was now apparent that McNab, for all his apparent failure, was undoubtedly in excellent spirits.

Then, as my own spirits rose, I perceived for the first time that we were not on the road back to Burrish, but, instead, were heading up the by-road that ultimately joined the road to Appledore.

"Where are we going?" I inquired.

"To get the keel, of course – where else? I have a notion that Farmer Holley can supply it, and so we're going to make a sudden call on him."

We walked on for a time in silence. Well did I know the mood he was in. He had divined – easy enough it must have been – my recent lack of faith, and in consequence would voluntarily explain nothing, but force me to put questions, like a child, at every turn.

"What is the keel for when you get it? Is that a secret?"

"No, it's not. There's no secrets kept from you, lad! You've seen all I have seen, and so you ought to know all I know. Don't tell me," he went on in mock indignation, "that you cannot see to what use I'm going to put the keel."

"I'm hanged if I do, and I'm damned if I believe anyone else could guess," I added, violently irritated.

"No? Why now, Godfrey, I'd have said any fool could tell that. If this were a lonely road in Scotland, and if I met a fool on it, I'd stop him and say: 'Look here, fool, I'm seeking some keel from a sheep farmer up beyond; what do you suppose I want it for?' What would he reply? 'Fool yourself,' he'd say, 'for asking such a question, for there's only one use I ever heard of for that stuff, and if it's keel you're after it can only be that you have a sheep or two to mark.'"

That simply stopped me dead on the road.

"McNab," I cried, "you know who the man is."

All the banter died from his voice as he replied.

"No," he said with great seriousness, "no, I do not. What I told you, when we traced Todd's trickery with that letter, was that I had a glimmer. Well, it has grown since then, by what we learned this afternoon." He laid his hand on my arm. "But tonight I think we'll learn not only who he is, but – something quite as essential – how he did it."

"Tonight?"

"Yes, tonight – when we spring our simple little trap."

Chapter 19

When we reached the Woolpack after getting the red keel from Holley I was ready to work on with the blindest faith in McNab. He warned me we were in for a dangerous night, a night in which death, in a strange form, might come in search of us. A certain amount of fear I saw he had, but no flinching from his purpose. Yet he grew more restless after sunset. Before it was quite dark he took the bag of red keel and went out on to the garden behind the house. From my bedroom window I could just discern him, bag in hand, scattering the red powder over a wide area between the house and the dyke. By the time he had emptied his bag I could no longer see him. But I heard him mount the stairs. He came straight to my room and beckoned me with a hand dyed red, as if with blood.

When I entered his own room he was washing off the stains.

"No use hoping for footprints tomorrow," he said. "Grass takes no footprints; but that stuff, with the heavy dew to wet it, will colour the shoes all right. A good notion, don't you think?" he asked, with a touch of pride, as he went on scrubbing.

"Shoes always seem to crop up in this case," I said.

"Ay – and windows too. Cardew latterly shut his, but we'll open mine" – he nodded as he dried his hands – "when we've got it ready."

What getting the window ready meant I soon discovered. First, he let down the roller blind, and, while I held it so that no one outside could see, he produced a cold-steel chisel and prised out the slat of wood which covers the suspending cord and its weight. The cord, once exposed, he cut it through with a knife, and then removed the heavy iron weight. When the slat was replaced, the same operation was performed on the weight on the other side. Then, while I held the window up, and the blind down, he produced a stick to which a long length of rope, thin but strong, was attached. Once he had inserted this between the window sill and the lower edge of the raised window I began to see what all this meant. I saw, anyhow, that the lower half of the window, from which the weights had been severed, would come down with a rush the moment that stick was pulled away by the line to which it was attached. And the line was long enough to permit this being done from the other side of the big room.

But we were not finished yet. I was sent to fetch the pillows from my bed. I returned to find he had pushed his own bed close up to the window. My pillows he inserted longitudinally in the bed, and, the sheets being again pulled up, the bed then appeared to have an occupant asleep in it. Over the head of the bed he took the long line of cord to a chair placed against the further wall, and to the leg of the chair he loosely tied the end of his cord.

"This is your chair, Godfrey," he said. "You will sit here. When I signal you pull hard on this and bring the window down."

"It will come down all right, but where will you be?" I asked.

He indicated a chair some feet away from the foot of the bed, and a foot or so beyond the further side of the window.

"On that chair – with this torch."

From his pocket he brought out his heavy electric torch. As he placed it on his chair I was struck by the way in which so many of the odd articles already associated with the crime seemed to be again coming into use.

"Sure the battery is still there?" I said.

In response he flashed the light round the room. "There are two of *us*, you know. And you can have the candle for use after the window's down. That's everything, I think – except the waiting," he added, after a careful look round. Then we went out, leaving the room in darkness.

But once downstairs again I thought the time ripe for a question or two. My curiosity was at fever heat and far beyond suppression. Yet he evidently did not propose to explain anything. For, having drawn the lamp close to the armchair, he picked up his *Alice in Wonderland* and, with his pipe going, settled down to read.

"McNab," I said, "you expect someone to enter your room by that window?"

"Someone or something," he replied, without raising his eyes.

"You don't know who?"

He looked away.

"No, nor what."

"Or when?"

"It will be any time after ten, when the tap room has emptied and the place is quiet."

I glanced at the clock: it was not yet nine. His eyes had returned to his book. But I couldn't let it rest at that. I had to talk.

"Can't you be a little more explicit?" I urged.

He laid the book on his knees.

"Godfrey, I don't want to talk about it – not now, at least. I don't want to think about it – yet. But surely you can see for yourself what we are trying for. Take the very first facts Ann Cardew mentioned that first night in my room: her father's closed window, the top-dressed lawn, and his fear at night. Don't you see now an attack had been made on him, an attack which failed and, in failing, left him aware of his danger, but ignorant of how it had been carried out. After that, as we know, he bolted his windows and was safe – till the urgency of the letter he wrote to Todd took him out in the dark. Very well—"

"But the letter was merely to request Todd's return," I objected. "Where was the urgency?"

"Pah!" he cried in disgust, "no one but Todd saw the letter; we have only Todd's word for what was in it But I'm not going into that now."

I left him alone for a minute or two; but he did not lift his book. Of course I saw he was offering the same conditions as had led to the attack on Mr. Cardew; but with the difference that McNab had top-dressed his lawn and left the window open, while Cardew evidently had top-dressed the lawn after he had begun to bolt his bedroom window at nights. But what I could not see was how McNab could be aware that an attack was to be made on us that night. And it was to prepare the way for a question on that that I said:

"Just a little bit frightened, aren't you?"

It was as if I had struck him in the face. He jumped to his feet.

"Frightened!" he cried. "A little bit frightened? My God, man, if you want the truth, I'm so afraid I cannot bring myself to think about it! And you want to chatter about it!" He waved his hand angrily. "Oh, go away – leave me! You – you – distract me from my book," he ended lamely.

This outburst was more revealing than any explanation. His imagination, in face of the unknown terror we had shortly to meet, did not need the stimulation of discussion; it rather needed to be held in check. And he was trying to hold his own imagination down by engrossing himself in the fantastic world depicted in the child's book he now held in a hand that trembled.

Without another word I left the room.

But how to pass the time I did not know. I certainly had not sufficient capacity for detachment to lose myself in a book at such a time. Opening my bedroom window gently, I peeped out at the night. Like McNab's, my window overlooked the ground behind the Woolpack. The moon would not be up for another hour or so, but I could make out the dark mass of the church, the tapering spire rising like a sword into the cloudy sky above the quiet, ghostly trees. The murky, scattered clouds seemed to threaten rain, but none had so far fallen, and the air was moistly warm.

Down below the level from which I looked all was in blackness. I could not see the dyke, which ran past the house out beyond the stretch of turf which McNab had top-dressed; but from its steep sides came the soft rustling of its tall reeds. The sound, familiar enough now, had struck me as strange on the first night I had slept in that room. The reeds on the dykes are never still. Even on the quietest night I heard the rustling, for the heavy seed pods, forming on their tops, make them responsive to the imperceptible currents of air that drift across that wide and bare expanse.

Behind me a board creaked suddenly. Coming then, it made me jump round, my heart beginning to race. Of course it was only one of those cracks old timber oak makes when affected by some change of wind or weather. But I began to feel eerie. It had been too like someone creeping up to my back.

I slid my window down. What I wanted was human company and talk, talk about anything, till the time of waiting was over.

So I headed downstairs and walked rapidly along the passage into the bar. The room was, as I expected, unoccupied. Voices, however, came from the bar beyond. From the kitchen, higher up the passage, the occasional clatter of crockery was audible, and, more continuously, the voice of Mary Beddoes, busy over some schoolwork – something in figures to judge by the monotonous way she counted, probably on her fingers. An unusual number seemed to occupy the tap room, for the acrid reek of many pipes floated through the half-open door into the unlit room. I sat down just to recover my grip on my nerves and breath.

It was comforting to hear those voices in the next room. Here and there my ear detected several already familiar to me; the loudness with which the men spoke, as well as Farmer Holley's fat laugh, told me how busy Ben must have been serving out beer.

"Yes, it's a fine thing, being clever," I heard Zacchary Moss declare, "a fine thing provided y' knows when to stop."

"Stop what?" a voice asked.

"Being clever."

"Reckon that ain't no trouble to you, Thomas Vidler," Zacchary said.

"What ain't no trouble to me?"

"To stop what you never began."

"What're you talkin' about?"

Some heavy hand thumped the table with a metal mug.

"Now, look 'ee here, folks," Holley cried, "what we was talking about was being clever, like the two gents from London what's staying here. So let's keep it on that, and no – no personalities."

Apps, the carpenter, lent support to this suggestion.

"Bein' clever's a gift," he declared. "It comes by nature, it do; it's not a thing they can larn yer at school, though they pretends as they can."

"But what I says is," Moss reiterated, with repeated tapping on the table, "you've got to know when to stop being clever. There's such a thing as being too clever, which is what some folks don't know."

"Here's one as don't know it, then," Vidler said. "You *can't* be too clever."

"I ought ter have said: which even some folks as *'as* brains don't know," Moss said pointedly.

"Now, now!" Holley said soothingly, "that's personal, that is."

"Well, then, let Tom Vidler be quiet. What's 'ee know, him that's got a head on 'im as soft as the Ma'sh, and as empty as this 'ere mug."

Holley shouted to Ben to fill Zacchary's mug.

Little Uden's voice next came.

"Ay, an old hoary place the Ma'sh be. Seen a thing or two, it have."

"'Tain't no marvel this young chap's come to write about it," Apps said in an argumentative tone. "Wonder if the young chap knows the old ancient saying about the five parts of this here world."

"But they don't print that in th' schoolbooks nowadays."

"You mean Europe, Asia, Africa, America and Romney Ma'sh? Ay, that were a queer way of putting it. Muster thought a lot o' th' Ma'sh in them days."

"Zacchary, you tell 'ern; he'd stand a quart for that."

Holley spoke.

"Ay, and I reckon Romney Ma'sh ain't the least queer of the five parts, eh, folks? To think it were once all under th' sea. That's a queer thought for a farmer, now!"

This set Moss off.

"Ay," he cried, "and what happened to all the drownded sailors when the sea walked off and give up its dead before the proper time? 'Twas onnatural, that was. Not till Judgment Day that shouldn't have been."

Somebody laughed shrilly. They all appeared to have drunk a good deal.

"But you mark my words," Zacchary Moss added, "you mark my words, the sea will come back, so 'twill. It will come back over the Ma'sh some night, and great goggle-eyed fishes will be a-looking in at folks' windows in the morning. All the dykes be a-waiting for the sea. I know! You can hear them talkin' and complaining at night. Always grumbling, the dyke water be, like an old man talking to himself of his great days of old."

"Ben," Uden cried, "we ain't got no matches."

"Two boxes on parlour chimbley, Mr. Uden," the busy Ben replied.

Almost before I had jumped to my feet the door opened and Uden stumbled in. At first he didn't see me. But the one thing left for me to do was to walk into the tap room as if I had been on my way there. They were all too far gone to mind my presence, and I was glad enough to be in the lighted room, for I didn't at all care for Moss's suggestion about the goggle-eyed monsters staring in at the windows. As I sat in the dark room alone, knowing what I did know, I wouldn't have turned to look at the window for a good deal, silly as was the picture conjured up by the drunken imagination of the gravedigger. But Mr. Apps was bold enough to question me.

"Be it about the smuggling days you're a-writing of?" he inquired.

That started them off in chorus.

"Ah, them were the wild days!" Vidler cut in.

"So they were, when men died bloody on the Ma'sh – heaps on 'em."

"And long afore them the Romans was here. Great Cæsar and his men of Rome, with their ships tied up at Lympne, when it were a harbour."

"But they were turned out too," Zacchary roared. "No popery, no popery! That's what I tell passen: no popery, or, you mark my words, I tell 'un, you mark my words, passen, I says, the sea will be over 'ee again, like as the Red Sea swept over the Eyegyptians of old."

Farmer Holley turned to a man I had not seen before, a youngish man in a sort of chauffeur's rig-out.

"You folk at Rye, now, wi' all your houses on a hill, you'll reckon yourselves safe there," he said.

The man looked at me and laughed.

"Well, sir," he said, "if you see things as Father Noah here sees them, your Guide to Romney Marsh ought to pay its way all right."

"He don't see things like me," Moss shouted. "Over sixty years I've watched th' Ma'sh, and nobody sees her like me."

"Zacchary most often sees things double, mister," Vidler explained. "Comes o' living so nigh the Woolpack."

There was a general cackle, in which Moss did not join. Uden felt constrained to apologise to me.

"Don't 'ee mind him, mister. Zacchary do go on like that when distempered wi' beer."

The end came suddenly. I had forgotten time. But now young Ben reminded us all of its passage. He knocked loudly on the counter.

"Ten o'clock, gents," he announced.

There was a shuffling of feet and chairs. Slowly, one by one, the company got on its feet and, more slowly, filed out through the tap room door. Ben too stepped outside to see what the night was like.

I made my way back through the bar, along the passage, towards our sitting room. But in the hall I had, somehow, to pause when, after a preliminary whirring, the clock began to strike. Standing there, I heard the separating members of the company shout their various leave-takings as they took their different roads home. The voices passed on and gradually faded out of hearing. Ben came inside.

The night was so still that I heard the key turn as he locked the door.

Chapter 20

With the clock striking ten that night there began for me an experience which, while it lasted, I felt could only have been paralleled by my prehistoric ancestors. The emotions awakened as I sat in the dark on that chair in McNab's room belonged properly to the Stone Age. Some ancestor of mine, ignorant, imaginative and ill-equipped for self-defence, who barricaded himself in his cave at nightfall from the terrors that moved around him in the darkness – he must have felt all that I felt that night. It is the unknown that really terrifies, and probably what re-echoed in my blood then came out of some experience of a prehistoric ancestor who feared much because he knew so little.

For as I sat there waiting, with the end of that line in one hand and McNab's electric torch ready in the other, I did not know for what I waited. Even McNab himself did not know; he merely suspected. His measures had been taken with the object of trapping whatever entered that room, but he did not know whether what we waited for was a person or a thing. That it would approach on feet he did expect, as I saw from the use he had made of the red powdered keel. But how was the room to be reached in the manner he expected – so noiseless that he had forbidden me to move, or even to whisper? A descent to the window could be made from the roof; the window could be reached from the ground by a ladder of moderate length, but by neither method could the room have been entered noiselessly.

Yet he was so certain this could, and would, be the case that he had forbidden me not only speech, but movement.

And then I saw another thing. McNab thought that whoever or whatever entered by that window could also leave it with equal speed and silence. That there was something unusual in this I became more certain as time wore on. For there were two of us in the room, both physically a match for any ordinary man; taking him unawares, we could have him on his back before he knew he had been gripped. Yet the rope in my hand, set to let the window drop, the cutting away of the weights, which would let it drop like lightning and render it so heavy to raise again, these were precautions judged essential by McNab.

The more I thought of it the less I liked it. If only I could have whispered a word or two to lessen the strain of waiting! But, instead, I inevitably began to think of what had happened to Mr. Cardew and Hackett. Once more I saw George Jippling giving his evidence at the inquest. His eyes had been on Mr. Cardew all the time. And, whether on the road or on the lawn, Death had come to strike his master down – had come and gone unseen. As for Hackett, it was true no one had seen him die, but the significant thing was that Hackett had somehow come to know the danger; was, in fact, on the alert against it, and yet had failed to save himself.

"There will be no sound," McNab had warned me outside the door before we entered.

"But," I had said, "in that case, how am I to know when to pull the line and switch on the torch?"

He had decided that I must also manipulate the torch so that both his own hands could be free, and himself unseen till he got to close quarters with the intruder.

"I'll overturn my chair as I rise," he said. "When you hear that you pull the line and flash the torch on to the pillow."

All this I kept repeating to myself. But as I recalled what happened to Hackett's torch I wanted to let go the rope for one moment to reassure myself that the battery had not again been spirited away. If only I had known what to expect it would have been different. Even McNab himself, however, did not know that! And of course I soon saw he had assigned the really dangerous position to himself. My part, away at the back of the room, was almost passive. Sitting in the dark, I had merely to pull one thing with my right hand and press another with my left, while he had to go at once into grips with something deadly, the form and substance of which he did not know.

If only I could have stopped thinking about that! As the time passed my fingers began to numb, and I had to relax my hold on the torch and rope. My eyes, too, began to ache from the perfectly useless efforts to watch the window. McNab I knew to be sitting near it, to one side, close to the foot of the bed; but I saw and heard nothing. Through the open window came the coolness of the night air, and the dank smell of earth. It felt as if rain were on the way. But the thought of the rain falling on the thirsty land, pattering on the leaves, sinking into the hungry grass, made my mouth feel more parched than ever. Would the rain come in at the window? I tried to see along the line I held, the line which, passing over the dummy figure in the bed, reached to the stick that supported the heavy window frame that was to come down like a guillotine. What a horrid noise it would make after all this silence! But would that be the only noise? What was to happen after the window fell? Would someone scream? I hoped not, but prepared I must be if I was to hold that light steady on the object. My guide to the spot would, of course, be the rope which stretched over the bed; over, that is, the exact spot where McNab's head was supposed to be resting on the pillow. And *what* would the light fall on when that moment came?

At this point it was that I resolutely turned my thoughts into another channel. That effort I remember quite well. In fact, I ceased to think and began instead merely to count. One can hypnotise oneself out of thought by figures. Thoughts have to clothe themselves in words; and figures are not words. So I began to count sheep jumping over a fence, one after another in an endless succession. This was at first effective; the similarity of each animal to all its predecessors, and the monotonous rhythm of their rise and fall, drugged the brain into inactivity. But presently I found that my mind, as if in rebellion, had begun to introduce variations into the vision; the leaping animals began to vary in size and colour. Some were marked with red and some with blue keel; some had the colour on their flanks, and others on their necks; but above all, as they began to leap higher, ever higher and faster, I was sure that one of them could leap from the ground right through the window.

Then something happened that jerked me out of the hypnotic torpor into which I had sunk as a refuge from thought. I felt the rope being quietly pulled from my hand. For an instant or two I felt it going. I was perhaps a little dazed at the moment, vaguely feeling that this was the exact opposite of what had been arranged. It was I who had to pull the rope. Instinctively my grip tightened and, laying the torch on my knees, with both hands I held on.

Fully alert now, I felt no tug at the other end by the window. Had it merely been slipping away through my relaxed fingers by its own weight? Yes, I told myself, it must have been that. But what luck that I had just held on, and not pulled, when I felt the rope move through my hand, for then I must have brought the window down with a crash. Putting my released hand up to rub my aching eyes, I found my forehead cold with sweat.

Then over in the darkness where I knew McNab sat waiting I heard a chair creak, and my nerves went jangling again. Was the sound meant to be the signal? Or was it a sound inadvertently made as he bent forward to watch with more intentness? I could not be sure.

But not for long was I left in doubt. The next instant the chair went over with a terrible bang and a noise of splintering wood.

"Pull!" McNab shouted.

Down came the window with a crash.

"Now – the torch!" he cried again.

But I was not so quick with that. I had put it on my knees, and in my eagerness to tug the window prop away had let it slip to the floor. It was only at my feet, though, yet as I swooped to snatch it up a horrible sound filled the room, a harsh, hard, continuous grating sound, like the running out of a cable when a ship drops anchor. I went suddenly giddy with a feeling of sickness and nausea, more of the mind than of the body.

"Quick, for God's sake!" McNab cried as the sound rose in pitch into a shrill tearing kind of whistling. Then my hand found the torch. Leaping to my feet I switched it on.

McNab was bending towards the bed in an attitude of tense eagerness, an uplifted poker in his hand, ready to strike.

But there did not seem to be anything there to strike. The bed, so far as I could see, remained undisturbed, exactly as we had last seen it. McNab perceived this too.

"Ah, we were too late," he said, relaxing and lowering his weapon. "We were not quick enough; it has got clean away."

I turned my light on the window: down it was all right.

"Are you sure anything entered at all?" I asked as he struck a match and lit his candle; for it seemed to me that the evidence indicated we had been too quick rather than too slow.

"Did that sound tell you nothing?" he asked, holding up his candle. "Wasn't that proof enough that something had got in here?"

This I could not controvert, but to me the sound had been so much in the air, so to speak, was so pervading in quality, as hardly to be assignable to any precise position or locality. As I stood so thinking, while he peered about with his candle, I saw him pull up suddenly to stare at something on the window sill.

"Well," he said, as if to himself, "that's proof, anyhow."

When I went over he pointed. "Look at that, Godfrey," he said. "Isn't that proof this room was entered just now?"

On the window sill there lay a slug, which had evidently crawled in while the window was open. Slugs, I knew, were apt to crawl into houses off a mossy roof such as the Woolpack had, or from wall creepers, under the threat of approaching heavy rain. But it was not its presence on the sill that was significant. That would have proved nothing at all. What did prove that something had come into that room, and left it, was the fact that the creature lay there in halves. It was still writhing.

It had just been cut into two pieces, cleanly, as if by a knife.

Chapter 21

It rained all that night, a soft, heavy, continuous downpour. I lay in bed and listened to it pattering refreshingly on the virginia creeper near my window, and imagined how the hot, dry turf would be drinking it in. It brought a soft coolness into the parched air that I could feel on my tired eyes. It seemed to wash away the sensation of nausea that had filled my mouth and mounted to the brain while that thing was in the room. Rain, it is a clean thing; it comes from the heights, not from the depths, like the unknown horror that had come in the darkness.

But for all that I could not sleep. To banish from my mind the happenings of the earlier part of that night was beyond my power. At first I did not attempt to do so. What had entered McNab's room while we sat in the dark? No human being – of that I was certain; there had not been sufficient time, and it had been effected far too noiselessly for that to be possible. I had not debated the matter with McNab before we finally retired. A glance at his face was enough to show me it would have been useless: he was as much perplexed as myself, and I think we were both too tired and much too dispirited by our failure to talk at all.

It was a knocking on my door that awakened me. So emphatic a tattoo implied a previous attempt which had failed to rouse me. There was urgency in that knocking. I sat up and shouted the invitation to enter. But I had forgotten my door was locked, for the first time, last night. More than half ashamed of the timidity proclaimed by this action, I jumped from bed to turn the key. The opened door revealed Inspector Rawnsley. His nod of recognition was followed by a half-smile at my astonishment.

"They let me call you," he said. "If we can talk here it would be better."

I was awake enough now at all events, and, wondering what this early visit could portend, held the door open. My first act after that was to throw the window up.

"Bit stuffy," I said. "Don't usually have the window shut, but—" I stopped, not knowing how to go on.

"Oh, yes, it did rain last night," he helped me out. "I say," he went on, holding out my hot water can, which I now saw he had carried in with him, "you don't usually lie so long in bed, either. Let me see" – he felt the side of the can – "yes, usually you rise – 7.30 to 7.45 I'd deduce if my name were Holmes."

Rawnsley seemed in excellent spirits; jovial, in fact.

"And what time is it?" I faltered.

"Just 10.30."

He laughed at my surprised whistle.

"Things taken a good turn?" I suggested.

"Got it first shot, Mr. Chance. They *have* taken a good turn, and the last turn, *I* should say, unless we reckon the turn of the hangman's halter round the man's neck."

This stopped me wondering why he had sought me out rather than McNab, which is what I had begun to do. It also brought the razor I was stropping to a halt.

"Going to make an arrest?" I hazarded.

"No – made it already," he snapped jubilantly.

"Not last night?"

He laughed again.

"You forget how late it is already. As a fact, we took him at eight this morning, in bed." Rawnsley broke off. "Why, you've cut yourself," he said. "Sorry I sprung it on you with a razor in your hand."

"Who is it?"

"Robert Sneyd."

"Sneyd!"

"Yes. He came quite quietly."

I recollect turning to resume shaving my chin with the thought that I need not have been surprised. All along Sneyd had been the most likely man. At first all the evidence available had pointed straight at him, though latterly McNab appeared more and more to be digging out un-obvious evidence against Todd. He would not like this news. I had a notion that he was fairly convinced that, though Sneyd knew more than he would tell, Todd was the man.

"Does McNab know?" I asked.

"Not yet."

"Well, he won't like this arrest," I bluntly declared.

Rawnsley said nothing at first. Then in the mirror before me I caught sight of his face; he was looking at me in a curious way that made me wheel round to stare at him directly.

"You think he won't like it?" he said.

"Sure of it."

And I *was* too; for I knew how a premature arrest often kills off the growth and accumulation of evidence still essential for a conviction. Then Rawnsley, that curious, quizzical gleam still in his grey eyes, said quietly;

"If you put that razor down I'll tell you something."

That made me stare, rather offended.

"Don't want you to cut yourself again," he explained. And as I hesitated he warningly added:

"You'd probably make a worse gash this time."

I put down the razor.

"Well?"

Rawnsley nodded approval.

"I fancy you're wrong, you know, in saying he won't like Sneyd's arrest."

"Never was more sure of anything," I declared. "He'll regard it as a bad blunder."

"Well, that's curious, now. You see, we arrested Robert Sneyd at eight this morning entirely in consequence of a message he himself sent us."

"McNab?"

"Yes."

I left the razor lying where it was – and sat down.

"Go on, inspector," I begged.

Rawnsley's high spirits no longer needed an outlet in giving me shocks. He began in a quite serious, almost official tone.

"About 7.30 this morning Sergeant Strood took a phone call from Ashford. He at once recognised the voice as that of your – ah – colleague, Mr. Francis McNab."

"Ashford – McNab – 7.30!" I gasped.

"You didn't know he was there?"

"Didn't know he was out of bed. But go on; I won't interrupt again."

"Strood at once recognised the seriousness of what was being said, and, snatching up a pencil, wrote it down. It was a message to me, and here it is," Rawnsley added, producing a sheet of paper.

What I read was this:

From Francis McNab.

I advise immediate arrest of Robert Sneyd for complicity in the murder of James Cardew. It is my intention to swear an information at or about 8 p.m. today in the police station at New Romney, where the full evidence will be produced. Advise that at the same time and place statements should be taken from George Jippling, Percy and Cyril Campbell, Rowland Todd and Zacchary Moss.

"Is that all that passed on the phone?" I asked as I folded up the message and handed it back.

"Almost. The sergeant said, though, while he was finishing off the message McNab asked if we knew Sneyd had been out last night. He knew, of course, that we've had a man every night after dark watching the house from the bushes close to the eighth green." Rawnsley paused.

"Well?"

"We *didn't* know Sneyd had been out – not till I entered his bedroom at eight this morning. You see, I had to help him to put his clothes on. Fresh ones. Those on the chair were too wet."

"He *had* been out, then, last night?"

"Unless for a whim he threw his suit out of the window, he had," Rawnsley said.

"It didn't begin to rain till after eleven, anyhow."

"Yes – *after* he had gone out; there was no wet overcoat of any kind in the house. I had a good look, you know," he nodded. "Oh, we have a tremendous case already against him. We did get his fingerprints – a tobacconist took them on a metal match box, and we know now he was the man who laid that cigarette case down before Mr. Cardew on his way home."

The inspector rose.

"You can resume operations," he said good-humouredly. "I have no more shocks."

But I had one question:

"Did McNab say how he knew Sneyd was out last night?"

"He did not. Strood, who believed he knew better, was about to challenge this when McNab rang off abruptly, saying his train was just in."

"Then it was from the railway station he phoned?"

Rawnsley nodded. He looked up.

"What I was wondering is: can you tell me what additional evidence he is likely to produce – its nature, I mean? You know the line he has been taking, of course. You see, what we need is evidence as to *how* Sneyd committed the murder."

But this information I could not supply. It was not in my knowledge; it was, indeed, beyond my capacity even for guessing. From the inspector's disappointment I perceived that, though he put the question after rising to leave, it was the real object of his early visit to me.

"You'll have to wait," I said. "From what I know I am certain he's gone to get proof on that very point."

"It's a deuced long time to wait, though – eight tonight." I agreed with his sigh. "However," he added, "I've all these witnesses he names to fix up. That will fill up some of the time."

For myself, I had nothing to fill up the time beyond my own thoughts. I sat where Rawnsley left me.

So I had been mistaken in supposing last night's trap had failed. But surely McNab himself, at the time, thought so too! But had he also lain awake afterwards – lain awake to better purpose than merely listening to the rain?

My head was in a whirl. I sat on, not yet daring to put the razor to my face.

Chapter 22

In *La Verité et le Criminel* that eminent authority, M. Bastin, remarks on the amazing way in which that type of murder which he classifies as a crime of deliberation goes frequently to pieces. That a murder, deliberately planned, should baffle and perplex at first is inevitable. The murderer selects his moment, place and method; he makes at leisure the arrangements he judges necessary to cover all traces, and not till the murder is a *fait accompli* do the police know anything about it. Then only the intellectual battle begins – the battle, as McNab put it, of *insight* against *foresight*.

McNab agreed with the Frenchman as to the way in which a well-planned murder often goes to pieces. Once the criminal's intellectual foresight has been beaten by the detective's intellectual insight, even on quite a minor detail, the whole of his elaborated defensive work is apt to crumble up, like a mill-dam pierced by a trickle of water.

That is what was to happen in the case of the two Marsh murders. But it may be doubted if the murder of Mr. Cardew would ever have been detected had it not been followed by the murder of the police constable. That second murder was a purely self-protective act on the part of the criminal. He believed it necessary, and, whether right or wrong in that belief, it was a murder which had to be carried out hastily, with far less preparation and care than he had given to the murder of Mr. James

Cardew. However, the interesting question as to whether all McNab's insight would ever have succeeded had there been no precipitate second murder may be left to the reader's judgment. Here I am concerned merely to record the facts.

After Rawnsley left and I went downstairs, I found the news of Sneyd's arrest had already spread to Burrish. At first no one knew for what he had been arrested; but the wildest rumours were flying. One had it that the police were now also searching for McNab, who had eluded them. Zacchary Moss was said to have met him before six that morning, while carrying his milk from the farm, making off in a great hurry along the Appledore road. It was also asserted that I myself was in Burrish pretending to be a writer, but actually to entrap Sneyd, and that McNab had followed me there as Sneyd's agent. The authority for this was Udell, who asserted he had known it all along. Later in the day rumour got fresh material, when it was learned that both Jippling and Moss had been ordered to appear at the police station at eight that night.

In the afternoon I went over to New Romney to hear if there had been any fresh developments. The inspector was not there, but I saw Strood, who told me Rawnsley had been called up by McNab from Brighton. But, though the talk had been lengthy, he was not in a position to tell me what passed. McNab had done most of the talking. As a result, however, it had been decided to take the evidence and conduct the preliminary investigation, not at the station, but at the Woolpack. There were, Strood understood, certain points in the evidence to be produced which would be thus made verifiable on the spot.

How I passed the time till eight o'clock is a matter of no consequence. Those six hours I got through by a solitary walk to lonely Dungeness, where, seated on the shingle with my back against a fishing-boat, near the Pilot Inn, I got together the first of those notes on the Cardew murder, exclusive to the *Daily Record*, which were destined to startle a continent. The truth is I was feeling a little sore at having been left out of active service that day. In consequence my journalistic instinct reasserted itself, and as I returned to Burrish I was planning how to get through to my paper that night as soon as McNab had produced the conclusive evidence against Sneyd which he had pledged himself to supply.

It was so close to eight by the time I approached the Woolpack that I first ran into Todd, and then Campbell, on their way there also. Campbell nodded gravely.

"Been dragged in after all, you see," he said.

Trying to reassure him, I said the meeting was quite informal, almost unofficial, and that it didn't follow he would have later to appear against Sneyd in the witness box. I recalled McNab's word to him.

"Yes," he said, "your friend undertook to keep me out of the witness box, but Inspector Rawnsley gave me no such undertaking. And," he added, "I suppose he alone really counts in the end."

Todd here turned almost angrily on Mr. Campbell.

"What about me?" he said. "You will get the credit of being an unwilling witness, for it's known you have been kind to the young fool; but what I thought of him is well known, and if anything I say helps to get him hanged I may as well clear out of Burrish at once."

Campbell laughed.

"Wonder if that's what Cyril has done."

"Your brother?" I said.

"Yes. Hasn't come back from town yet. Hanged if I know why, unless it's to escape this business tonight. Well, here we are," he said as the inn hove into view. Then he added in an undertone to me: "Cyril was rather friendly with Sneyd, you know."

The informality of the proceedings was evident as soon as we entered, and I fancy both Todd and Campbell took comfort from the fact. But for Robert Sneyd, who sat apart, gloomy yet defiant, the meeting, when we entered, might have looked no more than a chance collection of callers who had dropped in to see McNab, callers who were just a little shy of each other perhaps. No one in police uniform was present, though later I learned that Strood kept Jippling and Moss occupied in the bar. In addition to McNab and the inspector there were present two others unknown to me, one a tall, broad-shouldered, clean-shaven man, obviously an official; the other a white-haired, pink-complectioned man of about sixty, with a quiet, dignified, magisterial manner.

It was the magistrate, Mr. Colvin, who, by a nod to Rawnsley and an almost imperceptible gesture with his hand, sent us all to our seats around the big table. He himself took the head, with Rawnsley on his right and the shorthand writer on his left. McNab faced him from the lower end, nearest the door, and with me behind him, while Campbell and Todd fronted each other across the table; Sneyd, at the inspector's request, dropped into a chair between himself and Todd. At the same moment I heard behind me a slight shuffle of feet at the other side of the door. McNab's ear turned to the sound also, and I knew that a police officer had moved up, presumably to guard our privacy. Distinctly, the proceedings had taken on a much less informal aspect.

But, after the cool voice of Rawnsley had called on McNab in connection with the information he was formally swearing, McNab, pushing his chair closer to the table, seated himself again in the easy, careless attitude which told me, at least, that the Cardew case held no more secrets for him. But elsewhere in that room there was tension that held us motionless as he began to speak.

After briefly relating the visit paid to him by Miss Ann Cardew, and the facts which emerged subsequently, and which had drawn him into the case, he went on:

"In a crime of this nature, where one moves from the first in an atmosphere of lying, deception, pretence, double-dealing and concealment, there comes a time when one like myself longs for truth and frankness, much as a thirsty traveller longs for an oasis in the desert. Inspector Rawnsley will know that thirst. Well, I am going to give what has been withheld from me – the truth." He paused a moment, as if searching for a word or a phrase. "Frankness – yes, I beg your indulgence, gentlemen – this is a moment when I can revel in it, even though I must be frank at my own expense." He looked over towards Mr. Campbell with a deprecatory smile.

"Mr. Campbell," he said, "you were my first suspect."

Percy Campbell almost jumped from his chair.

"What?" he cried. "What did you say?"

"Oh, my suspicions were soon dispelled when I looked into your alibi. You could not be in two places at once."

Mr. Campbell looked more than annoyed: he was angry.

"Really," he protested, "I had no idea—"

"Routine work," Rawnsley cut in. "No offence meant. The Yard did it for us, too, at the hotel."

Campbell sat back again, mollified.

"Oh, very well; but if I'd have thought—"

He made a vague gesture with his hand.

Rowland Todd bent forward, his little eyes twinkling.

"By George," he said, "this is more interesting than I expected! I suppose now *I* was the next suspect, eh?"

"That is so," McNab replied, "with this difference: my suspicion of Mr. Campbell here was momentary; with you it has been continuous."

Something like a hush ensued; then a little cough came from the magisterial Mr. Colvin.

"Need we go into this?" he inquired. "Aren't you swearing an information against a named person other than Mr. Todd?"

"No, sir," came the prompt reply. "This morning I said I was prepared to swear an information against Robert Sneyd as an accessory in the murder of James Cardew. I did not then charge Robert Sneyd with murder."

A few whispered words passed between Colvin and Rawnsley. Then Colvin nodded.

"Go on," he said quietly, and at the words the atmosphere of the room became, somehow, electric.

"Inspector Rawnsley is aware," McNab resumed, "that *prima facie* there was as strong a case against Rowland Todd as against the other. I put that to him yesterday morning in the police station at New Romney. That same afternoon the case against him strengthened itself remarkably. Omitting the points such as the dispute or quarrel with Mr. Cardew, in which the evidence was as strong against Mr. Todd as against Mr. Sneyd, we need take into consideration only those points in which the evidence is immeasurably stronger.

"Todd's quarrel with his employer was not, like that with Sneyd, an event of the past; it was alive at the time of Mr. Cardew's death," he pronounced. "The whole matter I found complicated, but, if we follow the history of the letter Mr. Cardew posted on the day of his death to his former employee, it becomes simplified.. This letter, Todd says, was supplemental to an earlier letter received by him at Reading, in which Mr. Cardew withdrew charges made against him. The second letter was, he says, an urgent request for an immediate return to Redcotes. Now observe what happens. This second letter, addressed to him at the Hotel Riposo, did not reach Brighton till the Thursday. But Todd left the hotel on his motorcycle some time before dinner, which is at seven, on the Wednesday. That letter is redirected to him, and reaches Burrish on the Friday; that is, on the second day after the death, and the day before the inquest. Observe that it is a letter to which Mr. Cardew attached importance, and certainly it was the letter that took him out to his death. Yet Todd, well aware of this by this time, if not before, destroys it the moment it is received."

Todd started up.

"I explained that to the police," he jerked out with angry contempt.

"You stated that you destroyed it because it was an apology and, as a gentleman, you had no wish to retain a written record of a quarrel now dead, or something like that. Do you still adhere to that explanation?"

"Certainly I do."

"Did both letters sent by Mr. Cardew contain an apology, then?"

"No. The first did; the second asked me to return at once."

"But you destroyed both?"

"I don't keep letters; and, in any case, I had already returned."

"Did you know of the tragedy before you destroyed the letter?"

"Of course."

"You destroyed it, knowing that Mr. Cardew was murdered while returning from posting it to you?"

"I did not consider it of any consequence," Todd said sullenly.

"Very well! Leave that for a moment."

McNab picked up what I saw was the copy I had made of Todd's letter to Cardew. "Here," he went on, "is your letter of the 5th to Mr. Cardew, in which you accept his apology, agree to his offer and tell him you will be back in a day or two. That letter, as the envelope shows, left Reading at 10 a.m. on the Monday, and was delivered at Redcotes on Tuesday morning. So on Tuesday morning he knew you were coming back in a day or two."

"He wanted me back immediately, if that's what you're driving at."

"But, if so, why did he wait from Tuesday morning till Wednesday night before sending that request?"

"He had not got my Brighton address, of course," Todd said. McNab nodded.

"Yes, that fact knocks off a few hours. But it still remains true that, with all his alleged anxiety for your return, he did not seek your address for over twenty-four hours after receiving your letter."

"Still, he did receive my letter, and that letter speaks for itself," Todd rapped out.

"Did he receive the letter – are you sure he did?" McNab said quickly. His voice became grave as he continued. "I doubt if Mr. Cardew ever saw this letter of yours, Mr. Todd; and I will tell you why. In his study at Redcotes I saw a neat arrangement of all his correspondence of recent date. Police work, that: the letters of each day in separate bundles, those Mr. Cardew had opened himself, and those which, having been delivered after his death, had been opened by the police. You didn't need to look at the dates to tell those Mr. Cardew had seen. He, unlike the police, slit open the envelopes with his finger, not with a knife. But the envelope of your letter, which I had seen earlier at the police station, was an exception. It had been neatly slit open with a knife. That made me think. Here, I said to myself, is one letter, assigned by the officer to the Tuesday's collection, which looks as though it ought to be in the Thursday's. It disturbed me, that exception. Why should Mr. Cardew treat so exceptionally a letter in reply to an eager apology he had made? It was the very letter you would expect him to tear open in haste, since that was his habitual practice, as my eye told me, even with bills, which most of us do not open with any marked alacrity. Yes, I was so disturbed I went to see the postman."

McNab stopped and looked at his hearers. So did I, knowing what was coming. They all had their eyes on him, but the sneer had died from Todd's face, and even his lipless mouth seemed blanched.

"There was just a chance the postman would remember. He would take particular note of the Thursday's letters, I thought, if he had any gift of imagination at all, since he would know that the man to whom they were addressed would never read them. I put the question to him. His answers justified my hope. He remembered there were ten letters that day. But this was curious, for in the bundle I had seen in the study at Redcotes there were nine only. Where had the tenth gone? The answer was, of course, that it had been assigned, on account of its postmark, to the Tuesday's assortment. So, without more ado, we at least can conclude that here was one letter which by some contrivance got itself passed back to appear as a letter received and read by Mr. Cardew, but which in reality was a letter delivered after he was dead. Now the question arises: where had that letter, delivered on the 8th, been since the morning of the 5th, on which it was posted in Reading? The answer is that it made the journey in two stages. At the Riposo Hotel they remembered quite well the letter that arrived on Tuesday for a Mr. Rowland Todd; for it had three peculiarities: the address was in pencil, the envelope had been left unstuck and, as the flap revealed, it had come a day in advance from the very hotel from which Mr. Todd had written to engage a room for that night.

"On the following day this envelope continued its journey by motorcycle. But with differences; for now the pencilled address had been erased; it bore the name and address of Mr. Cardew in ink, the flap had been stuck down, and then the top neatly slit open. Is that so far clear? Mr. Todd now had possession of a letter which presented the appearance of having been posted at Reading at *10 a.m. 5 Sept.*, and of having been already received and read by Mr. Cardew, if only it could be got into Mr. Cardew's study. Mr. Todd was equal to that too, however. On the Thursday he had a mishap at the door of this inn. He ran into the postman, who had the Redcotes letters in his hand – *nine* letters. But after Mr. Todd had picked them up there were, of course, *ten*."

When McNab finished no one, so far as I could judge, had any doubt as to Todd's guilt. Yet the man himself, shaken as he obviously was when the postman incident came, still attempted to brazen it out.

"A fairy tale," he said; "a pretty piece of patchwork, constructive guessing, with no foundation in fact. What are your wild guesses against the letter, which speaks for itself?" He seemed to gather confidence as McNab said nothing. "I admit getting a letter from Reading at the Riposo; but I deny the supposed monkeying with the envelope. That is simply guesswork."

Rawnsley spoke.

"I have seen the envelope," he said. "Once my attention was drawn to it, with the aid of a magnifying glass it was easy to detect the erasure, and even to read your name and the word Hotel indented on the paper."

"What Todd has to explain," McNab summed up, "is how he knew on Monday, September 5th, that Mr. Cardew would be dead on Wednesday, the 7th. That he did know this is evident, for otherwise the letter he prepared and planted so adroitly, this letter which was to secure his position at Redcotes after the death, would have been useless."

Then indeed the wretched man wilted up, becoming in a second a thing the eye wanted to avoid. In a queer, wry fashion I saw Sneyd smile. As for Mr. Campbell, he looked on Sneyd with eyes aglow, as if he had just found a long lost brother. He certainly was not sorry at the turn the affair had taken.

But McNab had not yet finished.

Chapter 23

"The next step is to show you how the murder was accomplished," he began. "It is a thing worth doing, for I believe these two murders are unique in our criminal history. At all events, I know of no parallel to the Cardew murder.

"The first indication of what was going on we get from the dead man's sister, Miss Cardew. She observed one day that he had begun to examine his shoes before putting them on. Her inference was that he had become nervous about his health, and was looking to make sure the shoes were not damp. Her observation was good, but her inference was wrong: one does not knock shoes together to see if they are dry. Plainly Mr. Cardew thought there might be something inside the shoes.

"The next fact came from Miss Ann Cardew. She took note of a change in her father's habits, significant in a man of his age. He now shut his bedroom window at night. She, too, at first attributed this and other small changes to nervousness about his health. But not for long. One does not need to *bolt* one's window to keep out the night air. Young Miss Cardew became alert and watchful. She soon saw it was something external he feared, when she discovered how on certain nights he looked through the staircase window. These facts, and others, she told me in London. I tried to allay her fears. On the very day she saw me her father was murdered. In the news item recording his death the top-dressed lawn was mentioned. And, hearing of that, I became uneasy. Lawns, as you know, are often top-dressed to protect young grass, or to enrich an impoverished soil. But an examination of the Redcotes lawn made it apparent the lawn could not have been so treated for either of these purposes. The suspicion came that Mr. Cardew had top-dressed his lawn with sand so that he might get the footprints of someone he suspected of following him whose identity he did not know."

McNab bent forward suddenly as all our eyes were fixed on him.

"He never knew who his assailant was. Even George Jippling, who saw him being murdered, did not catch a glimpse of the murderer. But mark this: that attempt which succeeded – after he had been drawn out of doors to post a letter addressed to Mr. Todd, at the Hotel Riposo, Brighton, to Mr. Todd, who had left the hotel at least three hours and a half before Mr. Cardew carried his letter to the post – that successful attempt told me something. It told me there had been two earlier attempts – one by means of his shoes, while the other came through his open bedroom window. It also told me not only that the assailant knew Mr. Cardew knew of the attempts, but also the incident of the shoes told me the assailant must be someone who had access to the house. This partly explains Mr. Cardew's reticence: he did not know whom to suspect. Anyhow, the attempt began from *inside* the house.

"The next factor to consider was the cigarette case. I admit I could make nothing of it beyond the obvious fact that it had been put down by someone to stop Mr. Cardew, by someone who had reason to believe Mr. Cardew would pass along that road about that time. But what I could not believe was that that someone was Sneyd; for, even though Sneyd knew nothing about fingerprints, it seemed incredible foolishness to use an article which must be identified when he could have used as easily something not his own. And yet, if Mr. Cardew came out unexpectedly, one lying in wait might snatch at the first thing that offered, and it would have to be something bright and shining to make it certain he would see it and stoop down.

"I could make even less of the stick thrust into the turf opposite the spot where the case was found

– at first. But in the dyke, among the reeds, I came on, among other litter, a piece of newspaper torn from the 'Late Final' *Kent Evening Echo*. Sneyd had said he went to Ashford for just that edition; and as my scrap was of the same day and the same edition, and as it is certain it is an edition one must go a good many miles from Burrish to obtain, it was no wild guess to suppose that my scrap came from Sneyd's copy. It was also my guess that the hole which had pierced it was made when it was stuck like a flag on the top of that stick by the roadside. But for what purpose?

That was beyond all guessing.

"And that was the position of affairs, so far as I was concerned, when the second murder occurred."

McNab stopped the flow of his easy, even narrative. When he resumed his tone changed.

"Here," he said with emotion, "I must pay a tribute to the work of the very brave and clever young constable who died last Monday. He died in the execution of his duty, and, speaking with deliberation, I say it is doubtful if this murder problem would ever have been solved but for his astuteness. I have called him brave as well as clever. He was; for, suspecting the truth, he went out into the open to test his theory. I could not do that. Instead, guessing what Hackett's theory was, I tried an indoors experiment with the help and support of my colleague here – an indoors experiment, you understand, because the risk indoors was infinitely less. You will remember that the two indoor attempts against Mr. Cardew failed. Let me tell you what happened. From certain hints I obtained from the torn page in Hackett's notebook I was able to invite attack. By the way, I'll have more to say about that note in his book presently. Knowing, from what seemed to be a 'window' attempt against

Cardew, and knowing too from Jippling's evidence that there must be something at once capable of rising to a height and something also which would be invisible to the ordinary observer, we fixed the window of my own bedroom so as to trap anything that entered."

Here McNab laid his hand on my shoulder.

"Then in the dark we sat and waited. Sure enough Hackett was right! The attack came – like a stroke of lightning. Yet, though the window fell instantly, the thing got away before we could bring the torch to bear on it, all that was left in evidence being but this – this slug." He produced a small cardboard box and exhibited the two pieces of the dead slug.

"Have a good look at it," McNab said as he took out his handkerchief to wipe his face. The box passed round from hand to hand – to every hand except, as I observed, Todd's, who sat inert and heedless. Mr. Colvin stared at it and then held it up.

"Slug!" he cried. "This is no slug; it's a karrit, one of the deadliest reptiles in India."

Todd rose from his lethargy as if galvanized into life.

"I have never been in India!" he cried wildly.

"No, but Sneyd has," Rawnsley said as he pushed him down again.

Todd, under the heavy hand, struggled and pointed at Mr. Colvin.

"And this old fellow too!" he cried in shrill hysteria.

Mr. Campbell laid a soothing arm on his shoulder.

"And my brother too, if you like," he said. "So that tells nothing."

McNab resumed where he left off, this time in his unemotional professional manner.

"It was incredible to me, till I considered the pros and cons of this type of murder. What were its advantages? On the one hand, no general medical practitioner in this country has experience of death from snake bite; if successful, and death ensues quickly, there is barely any external trace left on the body, so the real cause of death would pass unsuspected. On the other hand, there is the difficulty of procuring the viper and of keeping it alive, besides the difficulty of making contact, so to put it, with the proposed victim, and also the fact that if death is slow there is considerable swelling. Yet, after all, there is severe swelling when death ensues from a mosquito bite, or even from the sting of an insect. There was, in fact, just one danger. Neither mosquitoes nor insects remain with their victim after doing their work. Was that what awakened the suspicion of Mr. Cardew when the karrit was inserted in one of his shoes? Did it crawl out too soon, or was it too moribund to do its work properly? Anyhow, the attempt failed.

"Yet the strange fact is that the method which failed in Cardew's case succeeded with Hackett. Hackett, as we know, lent his torch late on Sunday night to Todd at Windygate. And some time between then and the night of Monday the battery was removed from the torch and a karrit inserted. The heat of the body while the torch was carried in the pocket of a close-fitting uniform kept the viper comfortable enough. But when the moment came that night when Hackett wanted to use his torch he finds it would not work. So he naturally unscrews the top – you remember the top was found on the road – and inserts his finger to examine the battery. And this time there is no failure. The karrit does his work and slides out of the fallen torch and off, probably, in among the reeds. Hackett, unlike Cardew, was in robust health, and did not die for quite a time, as the swollen hand and wrist testify; but on a lonely road like that he was doomed; too late he made an effort to get to his cycle. Yet while passing into unconsciousness he made that heroic entry in his notebook which has made detection certain. I am not referring to the apparent reference to the trickery with his torch, which was, of course, of the same kind as Todd's trickery with the letters. What I consider as the two facts of first-rate importance we owe to Hackett are those which explained to me how the vipers were got and, following on the failure with the shoes, the new and more deadly way they came to be used."

He stopped a moment as if to choose his words. Most of us in the pause became conscious of the strained attention with which we had listened, and relaxed or shifted our position. McNab turned to me.

"Quick – whisky for Todd," he said.

Todd seemed in a state of collapse. No one had looked at him, or heeded; they were waiting too eagerly to care. McNab now sat forward, bending over the table.

"You remember, Mr. Campbell," he resumed, "when we came to you seeking for the clue you had unwittingly given to Hackett?"

Campbell nodded gravely.

"I do," he said.

"You suggested that probably the '-ell' on the torn page did not belong to your name at all."

"Yes, so many words end like that. I suggested quite a number."

"And I, though not a poultry farmer, suggested one – *shell*. My word was the right one. What Hackett wrote was: *First the soft egg-shell gave me the clue*."

Mr. Campbell stared.

"I don't understand," he said.

"It's quite simple. Your incubator number 8 was being used to hatch out imported karrit eggs. That solved the problem of how to get the vipers. All snake eggs are soft shelled. They travelled from India quite safely, for, though soft, they are very tough, yield where another egg would crack, and they are, of course, very small."

Mr. Campbell was inexpressibly shocked.

"My God!" he breathed, drawing still further away from Todd with every symptom of horror and repulsion.

Across the table I saw Sneyd staring at McNab, his face turned to a chalky white. And I remembered the experiment Mc-

Nab had made in the incubator house with those torn scraps of cigarette paper, which I now know resemble the scraps of a soft egg-shell after a viper has hatched out. I remembered that, though Todd and Campbell betrayed no apprehension, Sneyd, whom we knew to be also an experimenter in incubation processes, had not been present: he had slipped away beforehand.

And yet if Sneyd now looked shaken and white it was no more, or not much more, than the other faces round that table now looked. Indeed, the condition of our nerves became evident the next moment, when McNab pulled something from his pocket and threw it on the table. It was only the blue velvet bow with the rubber band, but they all started back as if it had been a living, writhing karrit.

"That is how it was done," he said. "The thin rubber band secured the viper, while allowing it movement. Behind the ribbon were several feet of gut; behind the gut fifty yards of silk fishing line; behind the line an eleven-foot rod; and behind the rod a living devil." Passion had come into his voice. "I know something of fishing," he declared. "It was a great idea to use a fishing rod for murder. An expert angler can throw a line and land it on a sixpenny piece nine times out of ten. If you don't believe me, ask Mr. Campbell there." McNab smote the table with his fist. "Oh," he cried, "when in the dark in my own room I heard first the line and then the gut go whistling under the edge of the shut window, so fast that it cut the viper in half, I didn't need to ask how the murders had been done "

Then he turned to Mr. Campbell.

"It is true, Campbell, what I said? Could you land a cast of fifty yards on a sixpence?"

Campbell seemed to be disturbed by the excited question.

"I don't know," he said uncomfortably. "I've never tried."

McNab laughed lightly.

"You remember our little chat about fishing? Well, you know, you'll have to forgive me, but the fact is that after that talk I did take another look at that alibi of yours."

"You what?" Campbell cried, like one unable to believe his ears.

"I went back to the Norfolk Hotel this morning."

Campbell threw up his head and laughed too. He did not seem annoyed.

"You don't really tell me you did that," he said with great good humour.

McNab waved a hand as if to brush something aside.

"Do you know what deceived me the first time?

It was the complaint about the badly polished shoes. The manageress said to me: 'He put his foot beside the other's to show his own shoes were not as well done.' That misled me. I thought she meant to say the other's foot, but what she meant was the other's *shoes*. The other's *foot* was not there."

Mr. Colvin bent forward suddenly, his eyes narrowing under the grizzled eyebrows. "I don't quite understand," he said.

"It's simple, though. Two rooms were booked by Mr. Percy and Dr. Cyril Campbell for Wednesday, 7th September, at the hotel. The doctor arrived about six o'clock with his suitcase, and explained that his brother would arrive by a later train, as he had been detained at home by an unexpected business transaction. Later he dined and went out. About eight a man who looked like Mr. Percy arrived, also with his suitcase, and asked if his brother had arrived. He was told Dr. Campbell arrived at six, but had gone out. 'Mr. Percy Campbell' then registered and took dinner in the restaurant. Afterwards he in his turn went out. 'Mr. Percy' returned first, shortly before ten, going straight to his room. A few minutes later – this was decided by the night porter, who comes on at ten – Dr. Campbell entered and, asking for his brother, was told that he must have returned, as his key was not on the rack. He then took the lift to his own room. Oh, there was no mistaking the one for the other. The elder, it was explained to me, had abundant, crinkly auburn hair, while the doctor had dark, close-cropped hair and, having recently come from India, wore a light grey overcoat."

McNab looked at Campbell critically. "I am inclined to think," he said, "that that grey overcoat and an auburn wig did a lot of quick-changing that night and next morning; an hotel with a main and service staircase and a lift and two entrances lends itself to that sort of impersonation. You see," he added, "this time I ascertained beyond all doubt that no person in that hotel ever saw the two brothers together at the same time. One of the chambermaids claimed to have done so, and her story at first staggered me. It was about ten, she said, when the delicate doctor rang and made the fuss she had told me about on my first visit over the hot water bottle. She hurried off to get one from the storeroom, and, having filled it, was carrying it to the doctor's room on the second floor, which was 29, when she saw Mr. Percy Campbell coming along the corridor, his hat in his hand. As they passed he smiled and nodded a good night to her, he entering 28, while she went on to 29, at the door of which she knocked. It was opened after a moment by Dr. Campbell, who took the bottle from her. She remembered his coat was off." McNab, with a grim smile, added: "Yes, that did stagger me, till I went up to see 28 and 29, and then found the two rooms were en suite, with a communicating door. It does not take long to throw down a hat, tear off a wig, remove a coat step through one door and open another in one's shirtsleeves.

"Next morning the doctor, having impressed his own individuality on the girl, proceeded to emphasise his brother's by that complaint about the badly polished shoes. Yet so deftly was the trick played that the girl is almost prepared to swear both men were there that night."

All eyes must have been fixed on Percy Campbell. He continued to stare at the table for a time. Then just when the silence became unbearable he looked up with grave, thoughtful eyes.

"Your story is ridiculous, of course," he said; "but I've been thinking it out, and I can see that, logically, it will be very difficult to disprove."

"It will," McNab nodded with grim assurance.

Campbell, I remember, propped his head on his hand and, looking at McNab, said:

"Just as hard for me to disprove as for you to prove."

"Agreed – if it stood alone. But there's that difficulty about the railway tickets too."

"Oh! Will you explain?"

So far there was certainly no apprehensive tremor in Campbell's voice, and I fancy most of us were in a state of perplexed, uncomfortable suspense.

"You both left Appledore by the 2.5 p.m. with two first-class tickets, numbers 12065 and 12066, in your pockets."

"Well?"

"You did not foresee the tickets could be traced?"

"I never thought anything about it."

"No; but if you had you might have seen the difficulty of your position. The idea was that, while Cyril went on to play the double role in the hotel, you remained at Ashford, where you had to change trains – to go back by road to Redcotes that night. But what were you to do with your ticket when you left the train at Ashford? Give it to your brother to hand over with his own to the collector at Charing Cross? That would astonish the collector. He would remember the fact. And yet if ticket 12065 never turned up that was presumptive evidence the holder never arrived at Charing Cross."

Campbell nodded approvingly.

"That's quite good logic as far as it goes. Like the other, however, it is all negative evidence. I suppose railway people can lose or mislay tickets just as other people mislay handkerchiefs."

This hit McNab hard. We waited, still in uncertainty.

"Mr. Campbell," he said, "you have twice mentioned logic. Your use of it is for defensive purposes. I am going to show you how it can be used to extract knowledge from ignorance and wring certainty out of doubt. Call Zacchary Moss."

That was my duty, but I went no further than the door, outside which I found the constable. While he was gone, and I remained by the door, McNab began to explain.

"You have heard something about the experiment we made with my bedroom window last night. It had two objects. To find out how the thing was done; for up till today I had no idea that so small and so deadly a viper as the karrit existed. The second aim I had was to mark the man."

Rapidly he told how he had laid down the red powdered colour on the grass outside the window. Mr. Colvin looked deeply impressed, as was Rawnsley, by this variant for getting the evidence footprints usually supply. Campbell's face I could not read from where I stood, as he sat forward, his elbows on the table, with his chin resting on the back of his clasped hands. But I think I saw the tightness in the supported jaw and the mouth suddenly relax when McNab admitted that the heavy rain which came on washed out his chance of identification. Just then I heard footsteps in the passage, and a knock came on the door. McNab turned and signed to me to open.

"Here, however, is a man who can tell us something," he said.

Zacchary looked as I had never seen him – a little frightened. Sergeant Strood planted him before us.

"Mr. Moss," McNab said, "after leaving the Woolpack last night you came back, before eleven o'clock."

Whatever Moss had expected, this took him aback. He fidgeted uncertainly.

"Can't see how you make that out," he said, weakly defensive.

"I made it out from your boots when I met you this morning. You were there just before the rain came on, were you not?"

"From my boots," Moss repeated in slow bewilderment, "from my—"

His eyes travelled over the company to see, I suppose, if we shared in his astonishment. "I wasn't up to any 'arm. Not me! It was only a drop o' water I'd gone for, a drop from the Woolpack well, y'know. That really was only water I was after, and if anybody 'as said Ben Beddoes was likely to break the law and—"

"Did you not see anyone, then?" McNab asked.

"Ay, the gentleman as told you he'd seen me, of course. That's who I saw, though I did think he were too far gone to have seen me."

"What do you mean when you say he was too far gone?"

"In liquor, I mean." His eyes travelled round the table vengefully till they rested on the man whom he believed to have made suggestions against him. The dirty forefinger rose and pointed at Campbell. "Drunk as a lord you looked," he cried, "drunk as a lord what with that fishing rod in your 'and and you throwing a line at the old Woolpack as if it 'ad been a 'addock."

In the stony silence which followed these fateful words I saw Campbell's right hand go round towards a pocket. But Strood was too quick for him. As the chair went over the weapon fell somewhere under the table, and after a sharp struggle Rawnsley, kneeling astride the prostrate man, had the handcuffs on his wrists. The inspector rose to his feet, breathing heavily,

"Now," he said, grimly emphatic, and looking down at the prisoner, "I'll give you my word not to put you into the witness box."

Chapter 24

About an hour later four of us sat down to supper. In the interval Inspector Rawnsley had lodged his prisoner in the cells, and I had got through to the *Record* on the phone from New Romney. We got back to find that Mr. Colvin had stayed on, not so much for the supper as to satisfy an appetite for further facts. And these, we learned with satisfaction, McNab had refused to give, despite Colvin's attempts to pump him, till supper was over.

After supper, with the glasses on the table and our pipes and cigars going, we all had a sense of relief, of the lifting of a strain that the case had ended. And McNab warned us that while he was prepared to answer questions he did not propose to rack his brains or abandon his pipe to make a continuous story of it. We were more than content to hear his announcement, for we had each our own questions to put. I certainly had mine. But at first we all hesitated, waiting for someone else to begin. Mr. Colvin eventually, and rather like a man saying something he felt forced to say, remarked:

"Haven't you been – well, rather hard on these two young men, Sneyd and Todd?"

McNab replied with the promptitude of one replying to a question he had expected.

"On Sneyd – perhaps. On Todd – no! However, I'll leave you, sir, to judge. If Sneyd had been frank about the cigarette case how much trouble it would have saved us! Why did he deny it was his? Because actually by that time it was not his; he had given it to Mrs. Campbell. The row between Mr. Cardew and Sneyd had been over Vera Cardew, before her marriage, and *not* over Ann, who was then a schoolgirl. Cardew wouldn't hear of an engagement because Sneyd was younger than Vera. More or less in pique, she married Campbell. But when Sneyd came home on leave trouble began. Campbell got jealous. Then something happened that brought the other brother into it. Sneyd discovered that Vera, after all, was only as the moon to her younger sister's sun, so to speak. And Cyril had marked down Ann for himself, an arrangement which would retain all Cardew's wealth in the family, of course."

"It was a murder for money, then?"

"Certainly. And they tried to get rid of the Sneyd danger by fastening the crime on him.

Sneyd now says he remembers handling the cigarette case on the previous Sunday. Campbell got it, and the ingenious devil kept it clear of other fingerprints to use on the Wednesday. Sneyd admits he lied about not being at Windygate that night. He was, and left the *Echo* there. The young fool thought himself bound to deny these things lest Mrs. Campbell should be compromised. Besides, he's naturally of a stubborn disposition, that young man."

Mr. Colvin nodded.

"He was asking for trouble all along," he said.

"As to Todd," McNab went on, "there we have another who was asking for trouble, though not through similar foolishness. Todd, in fact, was an ingenious rascal who overreached himself. He got into trouble with his accounts and was dismissed. Anticipating further discoveries after his departure, he engineered that trick which gave him an envelope postmarked with a date *in advance* of the letter he expected from Mr. Cardew. Thus, while at Brighton, he could write a letter to Cardew which would *seem* to have been written before he received Mr. Cardew's second letter. Obtaining the information he needed from this second letter of Cardew's, he wrote his letter and returned at night to perform the last part of his trick with the postman. But, learning of Mr. Cardew's death, he snatched at the chance to do himself a far better turn by using the envelope for the letter we have seen, the letter in which he appointed himself manager with an increased salary. A clever trick."

"Very nearly got himself hanged by it," Rawnsley grimly nodded.

Mr. Colvin, after a few thoughtful pulls at his cigar, said:

"Surely he, more than Sneyd, deserved the shock of an arrest this morning."

"Deserved, yes," McNab agreed at once. "But he wasn't accessory to the murder at all, while Sneyd, in the sense that he was withholding information, did so far make himself an accessory. Besides, I doubt if I could have got Rawnsley here to arrest anyone but Sneyd at eight o'clock this morning," he ended, glancing with a smile at the inspector.

Rawnsley was non-committal.

"Anyhow," he said, "we were ready enough to arrest Sneyd."

"Excuse me, but why not Campbell right away?" Mr. Colvin inquired.

"At eight o'clock this morning I had no conclusive evidence against Campbell. But he had already concluded I, like Hackett, was getting to know too much. Hence the attempt last night. After last night therefore the position was that, while I knew Campbell to be the man, I could prove nothing. He might have cheated the gallows by flight, or by suicide. Sneyd was arrested early this morning simply as a bit of strategy, to induce Campbell to believe that he had been mistaken, that after all we accepted the evidence against Sneyd he had put in our way."

Inspector Rawnsley ceased toying with the stem of his glass and looked across the table at Mr. Colvin. Mr. Colvin bowed.

"I've only two questions," Rawnsley said. "What made you first suspect Campbell, and what made Campbell suspect you suspected him?"

McNab's brow furrowed in thought for a little.

"I think," he said, "the first glimmer came to me yesterday at lunch. Up till then Todd had led me on a false scent. But at lunch I saw that the item '150 feet' on Hackett's notebook *could* represent a fishing line of the usual 50 yards, and that this would go with the word 'line' used earlier on the torn page. Then I remembered Jippling's assertion that no one had been on the road when Cardew met his death, and I asked myself if a fishing line had been used. I knew well the distance and the accuracy with which a fly can be cast. After that the cigarette case and the stick placed in the turf came into my sight. The case was just the thing to get anyone to stop and bend down. But the case would be unseen by anyone on the other side of the dyke. And to make his cast at the right moment it was necessary to know when Cardew would stop. The stick would tell Campbell that, for it was visible with the piece of newspaper fluttering on its top. And I had come on a piece of paper which I now suspected had been used for that purpose. The chances were that that paper was part of the *Kent Evening Echo* Sneyd had bought in Ashford on the night of the murder. But who had used it for this purpose? Sneyd himself? Or Todd? These two, I had just heard from Miss Ann, were not on good terms. And I had just got a grip on Todd's trick with the letter. So I went to Windygate more with the view to find out if Todd knew anything about fishing than with any great hope of picking up the clue Campbell had given to Hackett. But the interview hadn't gone far before I began to feel uneasy.

"What Campbell's nerve is you saw tonight. But just think, Rawnsley, of the moment when you produced your half of the page from Hackett's book. What a moment for him! He knew already what was on the other half, but not till then what was on ours."

McNab here produced from his breast pocket a sheet of paper and passed it over to Rawnsley.

"There's the page as, from what has since been discovered, I finished it coming down in the train tonight," he said. "It will show just how Campbell's failure to tear the whole page out after Hackett was dead must have kept him on the rack."

We all went round to thrust our heads over Rawnsley's broad shoulders. This is what we read:

Mr. Cardew was murdered not by Sneyd as I thought. First the soft egg-shell gave me a clue. Then the fishing-line, but take care. Campbell saw me at the eighth incubator, and I knew there was death inside. It was odd my torch would not light. Take care of what is inside a case or shoes. Length of fishing-line is 150 feet.

"You recall how Campbell sat staring at our half?" McNab resumed. "To perceive that, after all, nothing on *our* half pointed to himself! Then he began to – how shall I put it? – *dovetail* his story of his interview with Hackett on the Sunday night into harmony with the words Hackett had set down, the 8th incubator becoming the 8th *green*, outside Sneyd's house, and so on. But when he said Hackett told him they were about to take a *strong* line against certain *persons* – that was the moment suspicion of Campbell awakened in me; for I had concluded from the '150 feet' – 50 yards being the standard length at which a fishing-line is sold – that a fishing line had been used by the murderer. Campbell, I thought, must be perverting Hackett's words consciously. Hackett had written *fishing-line*, not *strong line* against a certain person. My next thought was that, if a fishing-line had been used in the murder, it must have had something at the *end* of it. What? The answer came exactly at the moment Campbell, suggesting his name did not occur on the page at all, began to mention words which also ended in '-ell.' The word *shell* came at once to my mind, and I expected Campbell to mention it. Why hadn't he? It was the first word a poultry farmer might be expected to think of. Then as I waited

I put the word *soft* before it, and instantly I had the clue to *what* was at the end of the fishing line."

McNab, glancing at each of us in turn, waited, I suppose, to see light break on our faces.

Rawnsley saw it first.

"Vipers alone lay soft-shell eggs," he nodded.

"Exactly; and *that* was Hackett's clue. And probably what happened was this: On the Sunday night, after he had helped Todd with his ignition trouble, he still had to get that plate with the Sneyd fingerprints. And to pass the time till supper was over you can see him rather aimlessly strolling about outside. He looked inside the incubation house, and there he saw, near the 8th case, some fragments of soft shells. Hackett was a brainy young fellow. And he knew that fowls do occasionally lay soft-shell eggs. But he also knew that with a ground soil so full of lime as Windygate no hen there could lay a soft-shell egg if it tried. Then probably Campbell, coming out after supper, found him looking into the 8th incubator. And though he knew how near Hackett was to his secret, Hackett did not, as yet, know himself. But Hackett presently did a lot of hard thinking. He must, too, have lighted on that fishing line to have measured it. He was beginning to put two and two together. Some time next day he went back for his torch, which he had perhaps put down and forgotten when Campbell entered the shed with his own light. He wanted that torch for that night. Possibly he thought he could work out some connection between the fishing-line and the stick planted on the roadside. And what happened when he examined the torch at that spot you know."

"Ah, yes," Rawnsley agreed. "Of course, Campbell was at Redcotes that night. He saw Hackett's cycle lamp, saw it go out and, coming along the dyke to make sure the damned viper hadn't stayed on inside the torch, found the notebook, eh?"

"Quite," McNab assented. "And notice, even at that moment his nerve was unshaken. He knew better than to take away the book itself. That would have raised a question as to where it had gone."

Mr. Colvin, after a moment, reminded McNab of Rawnsley's second question.

"And at what point do you think he suspected you were getting dangerous?" he asked.

McNab replid briefly.

"When I used the word *shell* he got frightened. It was a shock that made him drop Hackett's book. But so far he didn't know I suspected him. I tried to startle him again by placing near the 8th incubator fragments of cigarette paper to suggest fragments of soft egg-shell. But his nerve stood out this time. Then I let him see, with Mr. Chance's help, how, from my habit of sleeping near my window, I could be got rid of that same night. So when the attempt was made I knew who had made it."

This seemed to content Mr. Colvin. He rose to his feet after a glance at the clock. McNab looked very tired. Rawnsley finished off his glass, then stood up, stretching himself.

"Actually," he remarked, "the man made only one definite oversight."

"What was that?" Mr. Colvin asked.

"That about the railway ticket. He forgot it had to be accounted for."

"Well, you know, I thought his suggestion that railway officials sometimes mislay things quite plausible."

"Not this time," Rawnsley added. "You see, our men got that ticket on his brother when he was arrested in London at 6.30 tonight."

McNab shook his head.

"A bad blunder that – to hold on to the second ticket," he said.

Inspector Rawnsley's eye twinkled as he stretched himself.

"They were both Scotchmen, of course," he remarked.

Mr. Colvin smiled.

"You mean they did things thoroughly? Yes. Just think of the way Cyril Campbell worked that hotel alibi – two suitcases, two pairs of shoes, one pair for each door, two sets of pyjamas, a set for each bed, two dinners and two breakfasts to eat! That was doing it thoroughly."

Rawnsley laughed.

"You've forgotten the two tips on the washstands," he said. "But perhaps he did too."

THE END

 Visit Oleander to view all titles and sign up to our Newsletter

The Fatal Five Minutes
R.A.J. Walling

*The Crime
of a Christmas Toy*
Henry Herman

Death of an Editor
Vernon Loder

Death on May Morning
Max Dalman

The Hymn Tune Mystery
George A. Birmingham

The Middle of Things
JS Fletcher

The Essex Murders
Vernon Loder

The Boat Race Murder
R. E. Swartwout

Who Killed Alfred Snowe?
J. S. Fletcher

Murder at the College
Victor L. Whitechurch

*The Yorkshire
Moorland Mystery*
J. S. Fletcher

Fatality in Fleet Street
Christopher St. John Sprigg

The Doctor of Pimlico
William Le Queux

The Charing Cross Mystery
J. S. Fletcher

Free Golden Age Mystery

Fatality in Fleet Street ePub &
PDF **FREE** when you sign up
for our infrequent Newsletter.

Printed in Great Britain
by Amazon